"Hey, no fair necking in the front in the age of bucket seats!" Bev protested. "What do you think, that I wanna use the gear shift as some kind of sex toy? Get in the backseat, you pervert!"

Andie climbed somewhat awkwardly into the back, and Bev followed her, falling right into her lap. They kissed. There was something exciting about making out in the backseat of a car. It might be cliché, but it still felt deliciously naughty, like they were teenagers out past their curfew. Bev undid the buttons on Andie's blouse, and Andie soon felt the softness of her lover's lips against her flesh. "Ooh," she purred, leaning back in the seat and pulling Bev on top of her. A light flashed in Andie's face which gave her a sudden understanding of how animals caught in headlights must feel. "Don't move, Bev," she whispered through clenched teeth.

A face appeared in the window, the craggy, stubbly face of a middle-aged man wearing a green cap emblazoned with the words *John Deere*. He did not look happy. . .

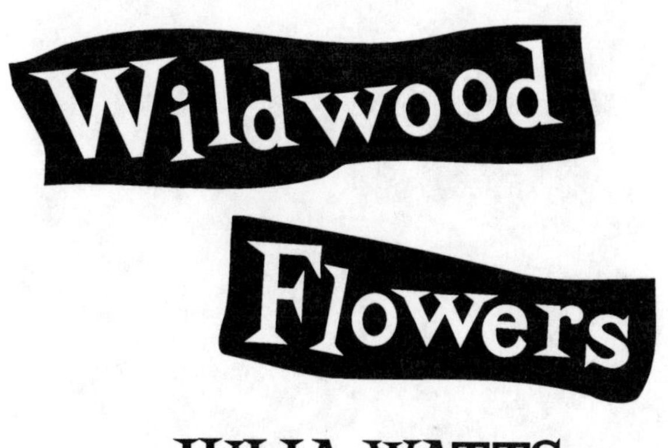

JULIA WATTS

THE NAIAD PRESS, INC.
1996

Printed in the United States of America on acid-free paper
First Edition

Editor: Lisa Epson
Cover designer: Bonnie Liss (Phoenix Graphics)
Typesetter: Sandi Stancil

Library of Congress Cataloging-in-Publication Data

Watts, Julia, 1969 –
Wildwood flowers / by Julia Watts.
p. cm.
ISBN 1-56280-127-9 (alk. paper)
1. Lesbians—Fiction. I. Title.
PS3573.A868W55 1996
813′.54—dc20 95-25878
CIP

Acknowledgements

Special thanks to Sena Jeter Naslund for her encouragement, the Kentucky Foundation for Women for their financial support, and Lisa Epson for her editorial skills. As always, my gratitude goes to Carol Guthrie and Don Windham for their friendship, Ian Windham for giving me enough time between diaper changings to write this novel, and my parents for everything.

About the Author

A native of Southeastern Kentucky, Julia Watts holds an M.A. in English from the University of Louisville. She currently lives in Knoxville, Tennessee, where she works as a part-time nanny, a part-time teacher, and a "the rest-of-the-time" writer. *Wildwood Flowers* is her first novel.

Chapter 1

Morgan, Kentucky, wasn't much to look at. Andie surveyed Main Street from the vantage point of the moving van's passenger seat. There was a Hardee's, a drugstore, a shop called Kathy's Kut 'n Kurl, and a restaurant with a filthy window on which Dixie Diner had been painted untold decades ago. Andie looked over at Bev, hoping to see some expression on her face other than the blank, stoic stare that had been there ever since they had crossed the Kentucky state line.

"Well, here we are," Andie said, for want of anything better to say.

"Yep," Bev mumbled.

Andie looked at kitty lang asleep in her cat carrier, zonked out on the Valium the vet had prescribed for the trip. Andie felt like she could do with some kitty Valium herself. She didn't know how to feel about this move. When she had gotten the call offering her the position of assistant professor of English at Randall College, she had screamed with joy the second she hung up the phone. Teaching jobs were hard to come by, particularly in the rarely-in-demand liberal arts, so she had to marvel at her luck in getting a job offer so soon after completing work on her Ph.D. That was the good part. The other part, the part about Bev, wasn't bad exactly; it was mostly just undecided.

Andie and Bev had met when Andie had been working at a women's bookstore in Boston the year after she graduated from college. In what was perhaps the longest courtship without cohabitation in lesbian history, they dated for eight months before moving in together. All through Andie's M.A. and Ph.D. programs, Bev had been the primary wage earner, working as the office manager of a women's clinic. Andie couldn't help but feel guilty. Now that she finally had a career of her own, was it fair of her to ask Bev to give up her career and follow her to — she glanced at the huge Baptist church that loomed before them at the end of Main Street — the ends of the earth?

"You need to turn right at the light," Andie said, slipping out of her guilt trip long enough to remember that Bev needed directions. What kind of person was she, making the woman she loved come with her to live in a house she had never seen in a town she had never heard of?

Andie had driven down two weeks ago to sign the lease on the house, leaving her little Toyota parked in its driveway and driving a gas-guzzling rental car back to Boston. Back in the city, the enormity of what she had just done hit her. Morgan, Kentucky, and Boston, Massachusetts, were about as dissimilar as two places in driving distance of each other could be. What if she and Bev hated it?

Andie had collapsed weeping into Bev's arms. "It's okay, it's okay," Bev had kept saying. "I trust you." It was the best and the worst thing she could have said.

They were driving outside the city limits now, and the feminine curves of the mountains swelled up around them on either side of the road. "The campus is out here," Andie said. Soon they came to a large brick gate with a sign reading, *Randall College; A Quality Christian Institution; Founded 1892.* A cluster of brick buildings sat atop the hill behind the gate.

"An institution, huh?" Bev muttered. "That's a good place for most Christians."

It was the longest sentence Bev had uttered since they had hit Kentucky, but it wasn't exactly the sentence Andie wanted to hear. "I didn't get the feeling the Christianity thing was going to be that big a deal. They hired me, and I didn't even claim to be so much as a Unitarian."

"Of course, you didn't say you were a dyke either."

"No, but I don't see what that has to do with my ability to teach freshman composition. A gay teacher can catch a comma splice just as easily as a straight teacher."

Bev lit a cigarette and opened the window a crack. "They've kept you locked in that ivory tower too long."

"Look, unlike you, I don't see what my sexuality has to do with every little thing. Take the time we took kitty lang to the vet, and you told him that she was the pet of a lesbian household. Do you remember how uncomfortable he was? And for what? What possible difference could it have made?"

Bev's fingers clenched around the steering wheel. "I don't want to do business with anybody who can't accept me as I am. Besides, if you're up front with someone from the start, you don't have to worry about having secrets later. For instance, what do you think they'll say at Randall College when they discover that you have a spiky-haired female roommate who just happened to move with you from Boston?"

Andie wasn't ready to think about that yet. She twisted a tendril of her long, dark hair around and around her index finger. "I don't know," she sighed. "We'll cross that bridge when we come to it."

"Excellent use of a cliché, Madam English Teacher."

Andie let herself smile a little. "We can always tell people we're cousins or something."

Bev stubbed her cigarette out in the ashtray. "Hey, what's the name of that bad Elvis movie — *Kissin' Cousins*?"

Andie laughed. "Like there are any *good* Elvis movies. Turn right at that trailer." She chose not to mention the offensive landmark that reminded her that the trailer was the correct place to turn — the concrete figure of a black-faced jockey in the front yard.

"Now what do I do?" Bev asked.

"Just keep going straight."

"Gaily forward." Bev never said *straight* if she could help it.

"Here it is, on the left."

Bev pulled the van into the gravel driveway. Andie held her breath as Bev looked at the white, turn-of-the-century cottage with a front porch large enough for two rocking chairs. There was space for a flower bed in the front yard and a vegetable garden in the back. In the side yard, a huge oak tree invited weary gardeners to lounge in its shade. Andie could stand no more of Bev's silence. "So," she prodded, "what do you think?"

Bev turned to Andie and grinned broadly for the first time in days. "I love it."

Chapter 2

The house was fabulous. They had placed the furniture in the living room, and Bev had just finished arranging the last of Andie's books on the shelves that lined the room's walls. At Andie's request, all the "controversial" titles had been shelved in the bedroom, lest one of the upstanding administrators of Randall College stop by and cast virgin eyes on *The Joy of Lesbian Sex*. Andie had insisted that they put a futon in the front bedroom, which she was going to use as a study, so that it would appear that she slept there alone instead of in the back bedroom with Bev. Bev was irritated by the closet Andie was building around them. But she knew how important the first job was to her and so Bev was determined to give life in Morgan a chance.

If nothing else, the house would make things bearable. After years of living in an apartment with the noise of tenants above, below, and around her, the sheer privacy of the country house was delicious. She and Andie would never have to complain about the neighbors' squawling babies or loud music, and they could make love as enthusiastically as they wanted without worrying that the neighbors could hear.

Andie walked into the living room carrying their framed print of Botticelli's *Primavera*. "How do you think this would look over the sofa?"

Bev took the picture from Andie and threw her arms around her, thinking of all the noise they could make together. "Not as good as you'd look *on* the sofa." She kissed Andie's neck.

"Hon, I'm all sweaty."

"So? I bet I can make you sweatier." She threaded her fingers through Andie's hair and whispered in her ear, "Botticelli would paint you if he was still around. You're so beautiful." She kissed her earlobe lightly.

Andie blushed like she always did when Bev told her she was beautiful. "Oh, stop," she laughed.

"Do you really want me to stop?"

"No."

Andie was sweaty, and Bev took great pleasure in breathing her musky scent, in stroking her sweat-sleek body. Her smell, her heat, was intoxicating, primal. Seven years, and the only itch

Bev felt was for Andie. Seven years, and still such joy sliding into Andie's satiny slickness until she felt, as she did now, the rippling waves of her pleasure. She would stay inside her for a while, she thought, wait until the pulsing stopped, then maybe start again. But a knock at the door made her draw back her hand like a toddler caught robbing the cookie jar. "Jesus! Who could that be? We don't even know anybody here."

"I hope it's not somebody from work," Andie said, quickly pulling on her shorts.

Bev opened the door to find an elderly woman whose enormous frame was zipped snugly into a pink-and-white checked housedress. Her thinning hair was permed so that it clung in tight little curls to her scalp, and her impossibly tiny feet were encased in white orthopedic sandals.

"Uh, hi," Bev said.

"Well, I want you to look at me just standin' here without so much as introducin' myself. I'm Mrs. Ancil Needham. I live right next door to you'uns. Course, everybody in town just calls me Mamaw Needham, so I reckon you can, too."

"Well," Bev waffled, wiping her still-moist fingers on her jeans leg, "Won't you come in? It's kind of a mess —"

"Of course it is," Mamaw Needham said, squeezing herself through the doorway, "What with you just gettin' settled and all." She shoved a covered dish into Bev's hands. "I was makin' this cake, and I thought you girls might like you a piece. Now I have to tell you, it ain't gonna be no good. Hit's just a box cake. One of these days, I'll scratch-bake you a jam cake so you'll know I can do better."

"How thoughtful of you," Andie said from the sofa. "We were just . . . uh, taking a break."

Bev suppressed a snicker.

"Now I don't believe I caught you girls's names," Mamaw Needham said, wedging herself into a chair.

"I'm Andrea, and this is Beverly."

"Call me Bev."

"Are you girls sisters?"

Bev felt fairly confident that Mrs. Needham did not mean sisters of Sappho. "No," she began, "We're —"

"We're cousins," Andie interrupted. "Why don't I put on some coffee? Bev, you make sure Mrs. Needham makes herself comfortable while I'm gone."

"I wish you'd call me Mamaw. I been called Mamaw so long I don't hardly know who Mrs. Needham is."

Andie smiled awkwardly. "Mamaw," she said, then beat a hasty retreat to the kitchen.

Bev couldn't believe it. Cousins indeed. She thought Andie had been joking when she had said that in the truck. If Andie had to lie about their relationship, couldn't she at least characterize them as friends? Cousins seemed kinky.

Kitty lang, who had spent most of the time since the move sulking under the bed, now crept into the living room to check out the new visitor.

Mamaw Needham eyed the calico cat. "Well, look at you. Ain't you purty? You come over here to me. Pussy, pussy, pussy, pussy, pussy!"

As angry as she was, Bev still had to conceal her amusement at a woman of Mamaw Needham's age and demeanor saying the word *pussy* over and over again, particularly given what she and Andie would have still been doing had the old woman not decided to grace them with her presence.

The usually neurotic kitty lang was settled in Mamaw Needham's lap and purring in no time.

"That's odd," Bev said. "She's usually so shy."

"I've always had me a way with animals." Mamaw Needham rubbed the nearly furless patches just above kitty's eyes. "My daddy always said he couldn't keep a farm what with me makin' pets out of all the animals. Besides," she looked down and addressed kitty lang in baby talk, "I dot me a dweat big wap, ain't I, pussy?" Kitty lang looked up at her new friend worshipfully.

Mamaw Needham was right. The cake wasn't any good. It was an artificially flavored strawberry number from a mix. Both the cake and the frosting that was slathered on it were the same shade of Pepto-Bismol pink as the checks on Mamaw Needham's housedress. Bev ate her big slab dutifully, commenting on how delicious it was, and noticed that Andie had managed to choke her piece down as well.

"So you girls ain't from around here, are you?"

"No," Bev said before Andie could construct some fantastic tale about their shared family tree. "We're from Boston."

"And what brought y'all down here?"

"Well," Andie said, "I got a job teaching at Randall —"

"I ain't a bit surprised you're a schoolteacher, honey," Mamaw Needham crowed. "You sure got enough books, don'tcha?"

"And Bev —" Andie added before Bev had a chance to speak for herself, "Bev came with me because she was tired of the city."

Bev suppressed the urge to roll her eyes. Tired of the city. Yeah, right.

Mamaw Needham smiled at Bev. "Well, I can certainly understand that, honey. I've lived in Morgan all my life, and I've never wanted to live no place bigger. Why Lord, all you have to do is turn on the TV to see how lucky you are to live someplace like this. Did you girls live together in Boston?"

"Yes," Bev said, beating Andie to the punch.

"That was a good thing, I reckon. It don't do for a girl to live by herself in a dangerous place like that." Mamaw Needham slurped her coffee loudly. "I bet the streets up there just run red with blood."

"It's not that bad," Andie said, sounding a bit shocked by the gothic description.

"You girls didn't leave no fellers behind, did you?"

"No," Bev said, so quickly that Andie glared at her. Bev was amazed at Mamaw Needham's nosiness, and yet she found herself unable to dislike the woman. For all her questioning, she seemed merely to be trying to be friendly.

"I'm not seeing anybody right now," Andie said, as though she was simply having a dry spell in contrast with her usual flood of male suitors.

"If you girls don't care, I might send Cricket over here one day. That's my grandson. He ain't never been married neither. I tell him the one thing I want more than anything is to have a great-grandbaby before I die, but he always says the right girl ain't never come along. You can't never tell; one of you'uns might be the right girl."

Not bloody likely, Bev thought.

"Course I don't mean one of you has to take to him that way nor nothin'. I just thought it'd be nice for you girls to meet somebody your own age. Cricket's a real good boy; he's head mortician down at the funeral home."

Bev was stricken mute. Andie looked dazed, but the corners of her mouth were turned up in a polite, if forced, smile. Jesus, Bev thought, we've been in Kentucky two days, and already one of us is going to be trapped into an arranged marriage with a mortician.

"Well, girls, I reckon I ought to go fix Ance his supper," Mamaw Needham said, dislodging herself from her chair. "Now if you'uns need anything, you just let me know. And if you'uns ever get lonesome and want to come over for a cup of coffee, I'm right next door."

"Thank you," Andie said.

"And thanks for the cake."

"Like I said, I'll scratch-bake you one next time." She turned to go, then wheeled around to face them. "Say, one of you girls wouldn't be interested in buyin' a used truck, would you?"

Bev perked up at a much more attractive offer than the hand of a mortician in marriage. She had ridden the bus to work in Boston, but it was obvious that if she were going to find work here, she would have to have her own vehicle. Morgan didn't have much in the way of a mass transit system. "Yeah, I might be interested," she said.

"Well, why don't you walk over and have a look at it? Hit's Ance's truck, but his eyes has got so bad he ain't got no business drivin'."

Bev and Andie followed their neighbor next door. Mamaw Needham's white aluminum-sided house was small and neat, with impatiens and bleeding hearts in green plastic hanging baskets on the front porch.

In the backyard they were met by a homely red dog who sidled up to them, tail and hindquarters wagging furiously. "Now don't you mind Bo," Mamaw Needham said. "He's the foolishest creature God ever let live, ain't that right, Bo?" Bo flopped on his back, his tail swinging back and forth like a pendulum gone mad, overcome by the joy of human contact.

The truck was out back behind the toolshed. It was an ancient Ford pickup painted a dull, faded cherry red. As soon as Bev saw it, she realized she had always wanted a truck like that; it was a dyke's dream.

"I always say that truck's like me," Mamaw Needham said. "Hit's old, but hit's got plenty of good miles left on it." She cackled at her joke, but then her voice turned grave. "Now Ance wants five hundred dollar for it."

Bev chewed on her lip and thought. She had two thousand dollars in savings. "Any chance I can take it for a test-drive?"

"I sure don't see why not. Let me run in and get the keys." Mamaw Needham waddled back to the house.

"You like it, don't you?" Andie asked when they were alone.

"Yeah."

"I could tell."

When Mamaw Needham returned with the keys, she was obviously amused about something. "Ance said when he put the truck up for sale he never dreamed in a million years that a woman would want it. I told him that this was one gal who looked like she could handle her a truck. Here you go."

Bev took the keys, climbed into the driver's seat, and unlocked the passenger door. "Hop in, little lady," she said to Andie. When Bev rolled down the window to assure Mamaw Needham that they'd be back soon, the old lady reached into the truck and patted her on the hand. "You look real good behind that wheel, honey," she said. "Only can I ask you one question?"

"Sure," Bev said. What's one more?

"Did you let them cut your hair that way on purpose?"

Bev ran her fingers through the short spikes. "Uh . . . yeah. We'll be back in a few minutes."

Bev and Andie sailed down the country roads. If Bev didn't blend in with the new territory, at least the truck did.

"Now you'll be telling me I have to let my hair grow," Bev said.

"Have I said anything of the kind?"

"No, but you did say we were cousins. That was enough. Look, if we have to be secretive about this, can we at least not pretend we're related?"

Andie stared out the window, feigning interest in a field of cattle. Her eyes were glazed over.

Bev could tell she wasn't going to be allowed to get anywhere in this discussion. "Wow," Bev said, purposely changing the subject. "I can't believe how little mileage this thing has on it. I bet they've never driven it further than to the grocery store."

Andie looked back at her, obviously more

comfortable with this topic of conversation. "I think you should buy it."

Bev reached over and squeezed her knee. "I'll tell you what, hon. I'll take the truck, and you can have Cricket the mortician."

Chapter 3

Andie finished hanging a poster of Virginia Woolf on the wall of her office. Virginia looked big-eyed and apprehensive, which was pretty much how Andie felt on her first day at Randall College. She had known the campus would be deserted today; registration didn't start until tomorrow. But the lack of human traffic was why she had wanted to come in to fix up her office and type her syllabi and inspect the classrooms where she would be teaching before she had to go about the business of becoming friendly with fellow faculty members and memorizing the names of countless backpack-toting freshmen.

Andie set her favorite coffee mug and a framed photo of kitty lang on her desk. A picture of Bev would cause far too much suspicion, but pictures of pets were always acceptable. She started a little when she heard the door swing open. "Ah, Andrea," a baritone voice boomed. "I see you're getting, ah, settled."

She turned around to face Dr. Paul Hill, the head of the English department. "Hello, Dr. Hill. Won't you come in?"

Dr. Hill was a short, stout man with gray hair and a matching gray Vandyke beard. Andie had often joked that you could always spot a male liberal arts professor by his anachronistic facial hair. Hill was wearing a tan jacket, tan slacks, and a tan tie. Were it not for his white shirt, he would have completely blended into the tan walls of the English department.

"So," he declared, waving a stubby hand toward the Virginia Woolf poster, "how does it feel to have, ah, 'an office of one's own'?"

Andie smiled at Hill's witticism since he was so obviously pleased with it. "It's wonderful, actually. My last office was a cubicle in a room shared with twenty other graduate students. Needless to say, it was impossible to get any work done."

"Ah, ah, I should say," Hill waffled.

Andie noticed that in addition to using the nonword *ah* as padding between real words, Hill also had the disconcerting habit of running his tongue over his teeth quickly like someone in a toothpaste advertisement. The tongue movement produced a highly biological slishing noise that sounded somehow too intimate for a work-related conversation. Andie hadn't noticed Hill's little idiosyncrasies during her job interview; she must have been too nervous. But now, as she considered the *ah*ing and the tongue thing, she found herself feeling grateful that she was Hill's colleague and not his student. She mentally shivered, picturing herself in a lecture hall making a check mark in her notebook each time he said *ah* and an X each time he licked his teeth.

"I, ah, think you will find our little department much cozier than the one at your, ah, university. We're a friendly bunch here, ah . . . Why, sometimes it gets downright lively here, what with everyone gathered around the coffeemaker talking about, ah, pedagogy and what have you."

Andie hoped the smile on her face didn't look too frozen.

"As a matter of, ah, fact," Hill stumbled on, "we in the, ah, department were going out together for ah . . . what?" He paused, and Andie wondered if she was supposed to take a guess. "Ah, yes. Lunch. Lunch at the Dixie Diner; it's a humble establishment, but it has its charms. I thought that might be a nice way for you to get acquainted with the department in a, ah, social setting."

"Sounds great," Andie said, already feeling her stomach tie itself into elaborate nervous knots.

"Splendid, then. Ah, twelve-thirty?"

"Twelve-thirty." Andie smiled again, she hoped amiably, and Dr. Hill pattered out of her office.

* * * * *

The first thing Andie saw as she entered the Dixie Diner was a metal stand by the cash register that displayed cheese curls, chocolate-covered marshmallow pies, and Sno Balls cakes. The delicacies were laid out, Andie supposed, as last-minute temptations for the customer at the cash register. As Andie stood at the *Please Wait to Be Seated* sign, she gazed at the chalkboard on the wall which announced the day's lunch special: KRAUT 'N WEENIES, W/FRIED POT., FRIED OKRA, AND CORNBREAD OR BISC. Andie tried to imagine all that heavy food dumped into her already nervously churning stomach. She hoped that the offensively-named Dixie Diner offered lighter fare as well.

A gray-haired waitress in a ruffled apron approached her. "You all by yourself today, honey?"

"I'm meeting a group for lunch."

"You with Professor Hill and them?"

"Yes."

The waitress pointed toward a table in the back of the dining area. "They're right back there, honey." She handed Andie a one-page laminated menu. "Here, you can take this with you."

Andie felt incredibly uncomfortable walking unescorted with menu in hand across the restaurant to meet a table full of strangers. Dr. Hill was seated at the end of the table near the wall on which hung a picture of two toddler boys in overalls and caps with the caption, "You been farmin' long?" Hill rose and grinned broadly at Andie, gesturing toward the chair across from him. "Ah, Andrea. Glad you could join us."

"I hope I'm not late." It was twelve-thirty on the dot.

"Oh, nonsense," Hill said. "As the, ah, man who jumped off a building said to onlookers on the sidewalk, 'I just got here myself.' Ah, everyone, this is Dr. Andrea Pritchard, who has nobly agreed to teach four sections of freshman composition this semester." Four sets of eyes were upon Andie. "Andrea," Hill said, "the lovely lady seated, ah, next to you is Dr. Nina Dupree."

While Andie found Hill's physical description of Dr. Dupree inappropriate, she had to agree that it was accurate. Nina Dupree looked to be in her late fifties and was beautiful, not in spite of her age but because of it. Age had bestowed the silver highlights in her ash-blonde hair and the striking angles of her high cheekbones. Her blue eyes sparkled with intelligence. She reached over with a rose-taloned hand and squeezed Andie's shoulder gently. "Oh, Dr. Pritchud," she chirped with a melodious, nearly *r*-less deep southern accent, "I'm so happy we'ah finally gonna have a *gull* in the depahtment. We'ah gonna have so much *fun*!"

Andie smiled and agreed that yes, they were. She wondered though, what exactly it was that girls in a lost-somewhere-in-the-1950's English department did for fun. Paint one another's nails and giggle about Jane Austen?

"And, ah, here beside me, this not-so-lovely gentleman is Bobby Adkins."

"Hey," Bobby said in a way that was obviously a greeting. Andie was more accustomed to hearing hey as a word that preceded a warning, as in, Hey, don't step in that! Bobby was a large, sweaty man in his early forties who appeared to be oozing out of his clothes. Sections of hairless white flesh spilled out of the gaps between his straining shirt buttons like bread dough that was just beginning to rise.

"If you have any questions about Randall," Hill said, "ah, rules, regulations, and the like, just ask Bobby. He did his undergraduate work here."

"About a hundred years ago," Bobby added, grinning sheepishly.

"And last, but, ah, not least, Dr. Pritchard, is our esteemed colleague Dr. Payne Symington McAllister."

"A plezha to meet you, Dr. Pritchud," McAllister drawled. Like Dr. Dupree, McAllister seemed to hail from somewhere farther down from the Mason-Dixon line than Kentucky. He was a handsome man who looked to be in his early sixties. Andie noticed that he wore a western bolo instead of a necktie, and she decided that he must be the "colorful" member of the department. She wondered momentarily if *colorful* might be a euphemism for *gay*, but then noticed the gold wedding band on his left hand that was identical to the gold bands on the left ring fingers of all the men sitting across from her. No doubt about it; this was a mighty straight bunch.

"I'm certainly looking forward to working with all of you," Andie said. Actually, what she was really looking forward to was going home to Bev and a beer, not necessarily in that order. She thought about Randall's strict no-alcohol policy and wondered which of her proclivities her tablemates would find more offensive, light drinking or lesbianism? That question didn't require much thought.

Her musing was interrupted by another shoulder squeeze from Dr. Dupree. "I know I speak for all of us when I say we'ah looking fahwahd to wuhkin' with you, too, Dr. Pritchud. It's just so excitin' to have a young puhson in the depahtment again — Why, Bobby's been the baby heah for I don't know how long. But to have such a young woman at Randall with such a sophisticated background! Why, you'll be such a fine role model for ouwa young ladies!"

Fortunately, Andie didn't have to reply because the waitress intervened with the question, "So what can I get for you folks today?"

Andie quickly turned her eyes to the menu. She had forgotten that there was still a meal to be endured.

Chapter 4

Bev had dragged herself out of bed at 7:00, showered, put on her best silk blouse and slacks, and even let Andie slap a little war paint on her. She knew that if she was going to find employment in Morgan, she couldn't fill out applications wearing her labyris earrings and her I'm-not-gay-but-my-girlfriend-is T-shirt. But she might as well have run down the streets screaming, "I'm a big dyke!"

She had gone to two doctor's offices and one law firm that had advertised for office staff in the classifieds of *The Morgan Observer*. At each place, a young woman with overpermed, overbleached, oversprayed hair had looked up at her with blue-eyelined eyes and droned, "May I help you?" Bev had smiled confidently and said, "Yes, I'm here to apply for the position that was advertised in the newspaper." Each overcoiffed young woman had eyed Bev suspiciously, then looked back down at her desk to avoid making eye contact while muttering, "I'm sorry, hon. That position has been filled." By the time Bev had gone to the third office and been met with the identical response, she wondered if she were going insane.

Now it was 12:30, and Bev was already exhausted. She stubbed out her cigarette and clicked off the TV. Nobody had even given her a chance to list her qualifications. She had a college degree and nine years experience running an office, and she couldn't land a pink-collar job in some quack's office in Nowhere, Kentucky. It wasn't like they were going to starve with just Andie working, but somehow Bev couldn't see herself staying home all day playing the role of devoted hausfrau. She went to the bathroom and stood at the sink, trying to decide which one of Andie's many facial products would most effectively remove her makeup. "Fuck it," she said finally, grabbing a plain old bar of soap. She was drying her face when the phone rang.

"Hello?"

"Andrea?"

"This is Bev."

"Bev, this is Mamaw Needham from next door. My grandson Cricket, you remember me tellin' you about him?"

"Uh-huh." Did she ever.

"Well, he come over here for dinner, and I thought if you was home I might send him over with a jar of apple butter."

Mamaw Needham hung up before Bev could say it wasn't a good time. What a day. No prospects of employment and a visit from a wife-hunting mortician. She had never met a mortician before. What would he look like? Lurch from "The Addams Family?" She didn't have to wonder long. There was a somewhat tentative knock at the door.

The entity Bev saw standing before her had none of the qualities she associated with the word *mortician*. He was tall and willowy and surely no older than twenty-five. His short, platinum blond hair was feathered back from a fine-featured face that sported an almost eerie Malibu Ken tan. He wore a salmon pink silk shirt, crisp white slacks, and boat shoes the exact same shade of salmon as his shirt. A jar of apple butter was held in his outstretched, fine-boned hand. Bev's brain loudly pealed the "gay" signal. Ding, ding, ding!

"Hi-i-i," he drawled breathily. "I'm Cricket. You must be Bev."

"Nice to meet you, Cricket," Bev said, actually meaning it. "Won't you come in?"

"Here's your apple butter. You won't starve to death livin' next to Mamaw, that's for sure. You shoulda seen the spread she put out for me today — fried chicken, biscuits, gravy. I'll have to live on yogurt for a week to make up for it!" He surveyed the living room. "Ooh, I love that print over your couch! It's so nice to see somebody with some taste for a change. 'Round here, it's nothin' but plastic wall sconces and big pictures of Jesus."

Bev laughed. If ever there was a day she needed an entertaining queen, this was it. What a relief that she and Andie weren't the only queers in this burg. "Can I get you something to drink, Cricket?"

"No, thanks, hon. Mamaw poured me so full of ice tea I'm about to wash away. I don't know if you know how old country ladies like her make it, but they brew it real strong and pour about five pounds of sugar in it. Why lord, drinkin' it's practically a mind-alterin' experience!"

"Well, do sit down at least."

"I think I will, for a minute anyway." Cricket parked himself in the chair in the corner, crossing his thin legs primly. "You gettin' settled in good?"

"Well, yes and no. We're settled into the house just fine, but I looked for a job today and didn't have a damn bit of luck."

"Where'd you go, hon?"

"I filled out applications at a couple of doctor's offices and one law firm."

"Let me guess." Cricket closed his eyes and put a finger to his temple as though he were doing a mind-reading act. "They told you the position was already filled."

Bev was amazed. "Yes! Why? Do I look like some kind of freak or something?"

Cricket surveyed her cooly. "To some people, maybe. Hair's a little short, for one thing. But what it is mainly is they don't know you. You're from a big city, right?"

"I lived in Boston all my life 'til now."

"Boston, huh? Mamaw didn't remember. She just said you was from some big city up north. Well, bein' from Boston you don't know this, but here in

Morgan or in any other little bitty town like it, if you want a job or anything else, it's all in who you know."

Bev ran her fingers through her hair in exasperation. "But I just moved here. I don't know anybody."

Cricket uncrossed his legs and leaned forward in his chair. "Now, hon, you're just about to hurt my feelin's. You know me, and believe it or not, in this town that's not such a bad connection to have."

"Really?" Bev didn't mean to sound incredulous, but she had a hard time picturing this obviously gay man as a pillar of the community. She was surprised he could walk down the streets without being attacked by an angry mob.

"I thought you'd be surprised. Let's be honest, sugar. You're a smart girl. You're from the city. You know that I'm not exactly the marryin' kind, don't you?"

Bev shifted in her seat uncomfortably. "I thought maybe . . ."

"Oh, come on, sugar. I'm sure when you opened that door and saw me standin' there, you thought, why, that Needham boy is a screamin' faggot!"

"I would never use those words . . ."

"Of course you wouldn't, sugar. You're just as sweet as you can be. But you see, even though everybody can tell what I am — except my Mamaw, god love her, and I just don't have the heart to tell her. Even though everybody knows, it don't matter 'cause I'm a Needham."

"I don't think I follow."

"I'm a Needham. I come from a good family. My daddy owns the funeral home, and when he dies, it'll belong to me. My uncle Frank runs the grocery store, and my uncle Jim runs the bank. So even though everybody can see what I am, they pretend not to because they know who I come from. They can call me a fag behind my back all they want, but anybody who calls me that to my face is trash because I'm a Needham. Does that make sense?"

"I'm beginning to catch on."

"There are other fags in this town who aren't as lucky as me. They don't have the name that I do, so they keep their mouths shut and act like they're just waitin' for Mrs. Right. Or they do like that music director over at the Methodist church who says he never wants to marry 'cause he just wants to play his organ for the Lord. Girl, I could tell you some stories about his organ that'd put hair on your chest, and I ain't talkin' about the organ they keep in the church sanctuary, neither!" Cricket hooted with laughter, and Bev joined him.

"Lord, ain't I just the nastiest thing?" He wiped his eyes with a hanky he took out of his pants pocket. "Anyway, we were gonna find you a job. What did you do before you moved to this godforsaken place?"

"I was the office manager of a women's clinic."

"Lord, girl, I hope you didn't tell them that at any of the places you went to today. That'd get you labeled a baby killer for sure!"

"Don't worry. They didn't give me a chance to list my qualifications."

Cricket clapped his hands suddenly. "Hey, I just had an idea. There's this place in town called the Mountain Women's Outreach Center. They run a thrift store and teach GED classes, classes for unwed mothers, that kinda thing. Daddy thinks they're a bunch of busybody do-gooders, but they're really awful sweet. There's a girl that works over there I went to high school with, Michelle. And it seems like she told me the other day that one of their girls was quittin' to have a baby."

Bev mentally crossed her fingers. Was it possible that she could actually find not only employment, but meaningful employment? "That sounds great."

"Fabulous. You can be a do-gooder then. I'll just call Michelle when I get back to work and tell her my good friend Beverly — what's your last name?"

"Jennings."

"My good friend Beverly Jennings who just moved into town is in need of employment and has an impressive record of work dealing with women's causes. How's that sound?"

"Cricket, you're amazing."

"I like to think so. You call the center later this afternoon, and ask for Michelle. I can guaran-damn-tee you'll at least get an interview. And you'll probly get the job. To be honest, not many girls want to work there. The pay's lousy, and the people who work there are kinda like outsiders."

"It sounds perfect. The pay doesn't have to be great; I need something to keep me busy. Can Andie and I at least cook you dinner for this?"

"I'd love it. There's no better way of thankin' me than puttin' me off of my diet."

Bev wondered if Cricket felt terribly alone being the only openly gay man in Morgan. There might be a better way of thanking him than putting him off his diet. "Look, Cricket," she began, "I don't know if I should be telling you this, but I'm going to anyway."

Cricket wrinkled his tan brow in concern. "What is it, sugar?"

"I'm not the marrying kind either."

"Really?" He squealed with delight and ran across the room to hug her. "That's fabulous! I thought you might be, but I wasn't gonna say anything."

"Yeah, Andie and I are . . . together."

"Really? Mamaw Needham told me y'all were cousins, bless her old heart."

"That's because Andie told her we were cousins. She's teaching at Randall, so she doesn't want anybody to know."

"Lord, I went there a semester before I decided to go up to Lexington to mortician school. Randall's no home for homos, I'll tell you that."

The danger of what she had just done suddenly hit Bev. "You won't tell anyone, will you, Cricket?"

"Sugar, don't you worry about a thing. Nobody can keep a secret like a small-town faggot!"

"Thanks for everything, Cricket."

"It's nothin'. You just call the Mountain Women's Outreach Center around three this afternoon, and I'll have everything lined up for you." Cricket looked at his gold wristwatch and bounced to his feet. "Lordamercy, I've done gone and outstayed my lunch hour! There was a bad wreck up on High Bluff last night, and they're bringin' in what's left of him for me to fix up. From what I hear it's gonna be like puttin' together a jigsaw puzzle!"

* * * * *

"I can't believe you got the job just like that," Andie said as she twirled strands of spaghetti around her fork. They hadn't had a chance to do major shopping and so were living on the few nonperishable staples they had brought with them.

"I know. It's really weird," Bev said. "Michelle just asked me if I could start next week. I don't know if it's such a good idea to hire somebody over the phone, sight unseen. For all this woman knows, I could have six-six-six carved into my forehead."

"Now, there's a good look for your first day on the job!"

"It was funny. When Cricket was telling me how much his name meant in the community, I couldn't help but wonder if he suffered from delusions of grandeur." Bev sipped her water, thinking of how excited Michelle had been that Cricket just couldn't say enough good about her. "I guess it's another case of family helping out family."

Andie dropped her fork. "You didn't tell him about us." It was a statement, not a question.

Under the table, Bev twisted her napkin nervously. "No, honey, of course not."

Obviously relieved, Andie smiled. "I knew you didn't. I'm sorry I even asked. I was just thinking what if he blabbed to his grandma next door. I'm sorry I'm so paranoid. If you had met the white-guys-over-forty club today at the Dixie Diner, you'd understand." She pushed her plate away. "Hey, I have an idea. Why don't we turn in early?"

Bev lay awake while Andie snored softly beside her. When they had made love, Andie responded with passion, giving herself over to Bev completely. Bev wondered if Andie could tell that she had been holding back. Even as Andie touched her, Bev's mind had flashed back to that moment at the dinner table: "You didn't tell him about us." Did one little lie matter, especially when it was told to someone who was currently living a big lie? Bev looked down at Andie's sleeping form, her hair spread out on the pillow, her arm draped around Bev's shoulders. Of course it mattered.

Chapter 5

Andie was alarmed when she walked into the central English office. Behind the desk that had been unoccupied during Andie's previous visits sat a middle-aged woman whose hair was piled into an enormous beehive, the likes of which Andie had only seen on particularly flamboyant female impersonators. The woman wore a Peter Pan collared floral-print blouse and large, round, thick glasses which gave her a pop-eyed, Boston terrier-like quality. She was drinking out of a ceramic mug with the name Joyce printed on it in rainbow colors, so Andie assumed that she was Joyce, the (she assumed again) departmental secretary.

But Joyce was not the one who alarmed Andie; it was the creature slumped beside Joyce. In a chair next to Joyce's desk sprawled a form that would seem lifeless were it not for the occasional shuddering snores that shook its tiny frame. In reality, the creature was not an it, but a she — an unbelievably ancient woman with skin as soft and wrinkled as wadded-up tissue paper. Her hair was hidden under a scarf that was knotted over her forehead, Rosie-the-Riveter style, and the lilac pantsuit which hung loosely on her bony body also harkened back to the forties. A thin line of drool trickled from the dowager's thin lips, which had been inexplicably painted streetwalker red.

Andie followed the line of drool in silent horror as it oozed down the old creature's chin and finally landed on the lapel of her lilac suit. Andie knew she had to speak; she couldn't keep standing there like an idiot. "Joyce?" she whispered.

"What?" she snapped.

"I'm sorry," Andie whispered even more softly. "I didn't mean to startle you. I'm Dr. Andrea Pritchard, the new assistant professor."

"Oh." Joyce squinted at her suspiciously. "I'm Joyce."

Andie didn't want to push her luck, but she had to know. "Who," she gestured toward the sleeping woman, "is this?"

"Oh," said Joyce, as if Andie were mentally deficient for even having to ask. "That's my mother."

Andie remembered reading that Flannery

O'Connor always said that her bizarre Southern characters were not exaggerations at all. She was beginning to believe her. "Is your mother all right?"

"No, she's not doing a bit of good, the poor old thing."

Andie was tempted to ask her if her mother were so ill, then why in the name of God did she bring her to work and make her live out her last days in an uncomfortable office chair. But she thought better of it. After all, she had come into the office for the sole purpose of having copies made, and that was exactly what she was going to do. "Joyce, could you please make me fifty copies of this two-page syllabus?"

Joyce heaved a world-weary sigh. "I suppose so."

The outdated copying machine, which was inconveniently located behind Joyce's mother's chair, made so much noise it sounded as if it were gearing up to take flight. The noise didn't make the old woman stir from her slumber though, nor did the fact that her daughter kept bumping into her as she retrieved the copies from the paper tray. Joyce seemed to be under the impression that each copy must be removed from the tray as soon as the machine spit it out, so for her, copying was an exercise in grabbing and stacking, grabbing and stacking, all the while ramming into her aged mother. The process had the appearance of some kind of demented Lucille Ball routine. Joyce seemed to lose her momentum toward the end of her task, letting one sheet of paper fall from her hands and flutter into her mother's lap.

Finally, she handed Andie her stack of copies. "You'll have to collate 'em yourself," she said.

Andie nodded, then pointed dumbly to the one copy she did not have, the one resting on the old woman's scrawny thighs.

Joyce marched over and snatched the paper. "Now, Mother!" she shouted into the old woman's ear. "You can't have that!"

The old woman snorted in her sleep. Joyce held the paper out to Andie. "Here," she barked.

Later that afternoon, during her office hours, Bobby Adkins stuck his head in Andie's door. "I was goin' to the coffeemaker. Do you need a refill?"

"Sure," Andie said, handing him her cup. "Thanks."

When Bobby returned, she said, "You know how Dr. Hill said I could ask you anything about Randall?"

"Uh-huh."

"Does that include questions about people at Randall?"

Bobby slurped his coffee and grinned. "I'll always talk about people. I was raised by my maiden aunts. It made me gossipy." Apparently sensing what was coming, he peeked up and down the hallway and then closed the door. "So what is it you want to know?"

"Hmm . . . I don't know how to put this, so I guess I'll just be blunt."

"Blunt works."

"What is the deal with Joyce?"

Bobby burst out laughing. "And a good question that is. Joyce is somewhat of an institution at

Randall. She was here when I was working on my Bachelor's back in nineteen and —" He purposely mumbled the year into his coffee cup. "She wasn't secretary for the English department back then, though. I'm pretty sure she was over in religion. The poor old gal gets passed from department to department like a hot potato. Before she was here she was in the ROTC office, but she about drove them crazy. I guess the president figured we English folk were more laid back, so now we're stuck with her. Joyce is sort of like this albatross that gets passed from neck to neck."

Andie laughed. "But what about her mother?"

"She's been bringin' her mother with her to work as long as I remember — says her mother can't stay by herself, and Joyce won't let anybody else look after her because she says they'd mistreat her."

"Whatever they did to her, it couldn't be much worse than making her sleep in an office chair all day."

"I know it. When Joyce was in the ROTC office, the major told her she couldn't bring her mother to work anymore. Then one of the ROTC boys walked by Joyce's car one hot August day, and her mother was in there snoozing away. Joyce had cracked the window for her a little bit, like you do for a dog."

"That's awful."

"It sure is. When she started to work here, Hill told her she could bring her mother. Told me he didn't want the poor old thing to die of heat stroke and have that on his conscience. That's the way it is with Joyce; you have to make all these allowances for her, when she's just a terrible secretary."

"So why hasn't she been fired?"

"And there's the rub. Joyce was hired by Dr. Arlington, who was president here for twenty-five years. For some reason — nobody's sure why — he liked Joyce and kind of took pity on her. So when Dr. Malcolm came in to take over as president, Arlington made him promise he'd let Joyce work here 'til she reached retirement age. Malcolm keeps his promise out of respect to Arlington. Of course, Arlington's been dead three years now."

Andie shook her head in disbelief. "That's the craziest thing I've ever heard."

Bobby shot her a big, gap-toothed grin. "Welcome to Randall." He glanced down at his worse-for-wear Timex watch. "Looks like it's time for me to enlighten the masses."

"Talk to you later, Bobby."

"We'll see you, buddy."

Andie liked Bobby. A local boy who had made good by getting a graduate degree at the state university and had come back home to share his knowledge, he gave Andie a fuller understanding of the term good ol' boy.

Andie also liked her students more than she had thought she would. At first, she had been taken aback by the lack of diversity. At the university, she was accustomed to teaching students of every imaginable ethnic heritage. And even among the white students, there had been diversity of personal styles, from the baseball cap wearing fraternity brothers to the tattooed and body-pierced bohemians. At Randall, the students looked remarkably alike. Except for the rare international or African-American student, they were white, conventionally dressed, short-haired boys and long-haired girls.

But these kids had a hunger which had not been present in most of Andie's urban pupils. Many Randall students were the first members of their families to attend college. Getting a college education had been a personal decision for them, and they were there to learn and do well. For that reason, they were inclined to listen to their professors, and they seemed particularly inclined to listen to Andie, a woman who was only a scant decade older than they and who didn't have the schoolmarmish quality they generally associated with women in academia. As one young woman said to her on the first day of class, "You sure don't look like a teacher."

Despite the fact that Bobby and most of her students liked her, Andie wondered if their feelings would change if they knew about her personal life. Bobby was undoubtedly good-hearted, but many people's goodwill stopped when they were confronted with something out of their frame of reference. And the students — the God-fearing, Bible-believing students, many of whom came from places with names like Troublesome Branch and Salt Lick — what would they do if they knew? Would they burn a cross in her yard or just pray for her eternal soul?

Of course, Andie had seen something yesterday that had given her hope that the spirit of tolerance at Randall might be greater than she had thought. She had stopped at the student center to buy a soda, and there, at the very table where she had once seen a faculty member chastise a straight couple for "publicly displaying affection," sat Dr. Dupree with the butchest woman Andie had ever seen. The woman's hair was cropped close and parted on the side. She wore a men's powder-blue leisure suit with a seventies-style wide-collared shirt. Dupree sat across from her, all schoolgirl giggles, fluttering eyelashes, and clicking pink-polished fingernails. Andie could hardly believe it. They were the textbook definition of butch-femme.

Andie had done little more than greet Dupree in the halls since their lunch at the Dixie Diner, but now she realized that if she had seen what she thought she had seen, Dupree could be a friend indeed. If she and her leisure suit-wearing friend were openly lovers, it could change everything for her and Bev. Bev would be so happy; she had a much harder time than Andie did squeezing herself into a closet.

A sticker on Dupree's half-open office door said, "I'd Rather Be Reading Jane Austen." Andie smiled to herself. She may have missed Dupree's sexual proclivities upon first meeting her, but she had definitely guessed her literary proclivities correctly.

"Dr. Pritchud, is that you I see standin' out there?"

"Yes. I was just admiring your sticker."

"Oh, isn't it cute? I picked that up at a conference yeahs ago. Why don't you come on in? I was just fixin' myself some tea and wishin' I had somebody to drink it with me."

"I'd love some tea. Thanks." Except for the desk in its center, the room looked more like a Victorian sitting parlor than an office. A pastel Oriental rug covered the floor, and dusty rose upholstered chairs replaced the usual bland office furniture.

Dupree was standing over the electric hot pot on

her desk. “Do make yoahself comfortable, Dr. Pritchud. I know what they say about a watched pot, but I always just stand right over it anyway.”

“I wish you’d call me Andrea.”

“Well, Andrea it is, then. And you, of course, will call me Nina.” She pulled out a desk drawer and produced two boxes of tea and, to Andie’s amazement, two china cups with matching saucers. “Now, Andrea, which will it be, Earl Grey or Dahjeelin’?”

“Darjeeling, please.”

Nina brought Andie her tea and settled down beside her, blowing daintily into her own steaming cup before sipping from it. “Now, isn’t this propuh? Heah it is, foah o’clock, and we’ah havin’ tea. I do wish I had somethin’ sweet to offeh you, but several students dropped by earliuh, and I’m afraid I fed them all my cookies.”

“That’s okay. I’d eat too many of them anyway.”

“You certainly don’t appeah to be a gull who needs to watch her figuh. You’ah just as fit as you can be. I was just tiny, too, when I was yoah age. Why, you could get both hands around my waist.”

Andie smiled. “Just like Scarlett O’Hara.”

Nina giggled. “Oh, that trashy book!” She sipped her tea. “Andrea, I sweah, I’m just so glad you came ovuh. We gulls have to stick togethuh.”

“There certainly aren’t many of us around.” Since she had walked into Nina’s office, Andie had been searching for signs of lesbian life. There were certainly things in Nina’s conversation that had subtle lesbian undertones — how she noticed Andie’s body, how she saw some sort of alliance between Andie and herself. Of course, those comments could just be written off to southern charm and hospitality.

"No, theah certainly aren't. Theah ah the secretaries, of course, like poah old Joyce. But women faculty and administratuhs are certainly few and fah between."

Andie decided to go for broke. "I saw you talking to a woman in the student center yesterday whom I haven't had the pleasure of meeting. I was wondering if she's a faculty member. She has short hair —"

"You mean Inez. Inez Ratliff. She used to teach health and physical education heah, but now she's the Dean of Women."

"Ah." As Bev said when she spotted a fellow queer, ding, ding, ding! "Dean of Women — that certainly sounds like a position of power." Not to mention a dyke's dream job, she thought.

"It is. You know, Inez and I have lived in the same house for thuhty-two yeahs now."

Andie nearly dropped her teacup. "I didn't know. Thirty-two years. Wow."

"We've known each othuh longuh than that. We met in college in Mississippi. Back then, you know, it was considuhed strange when a woman wanted to have a careah instead of get married and have babies. But that was what we both wanted — a careah, I mean. And we went off to graduate school togethuh, and then of coahse, we both found jobs heah, and, well, heah's wheah we've stayed."

Andie was touched. "That's just wonderful."

Nina seemed a bit taken aback. "Well, it is nice. We've always hit it off, Inez and me."

Andie took her last swallow of tea and thought

hard. She could mention Bev; she just had to proceed with caution. "I have a roommate, too, you know."

"Isn't that nice?"

"Beverly moved down here with me from Boston."

"Bevuhly — isn't that a lovely name? Just like Bevuhly Sills." She set down her teacup suddenly. "You know what I think? I think you and Bevuhly should come ovah to ouah house for suppuh Friday evenin'. That is, if you don't have othuh plans."

"No, we don't have any plans. Being new in town, we don't exactly have a full social calendar."

"Do say you'll come then. It'll be so much fun. Inez'll love meetin' you, and I just can't wait to meet Bevuhly."

"We'll definitely come." Dykes who had been together thirty-two years could be both friends and role models. If they were a little too into butch-femme role playing, that was understandable, given their age.

"Mahvelous! Oh, whatevuh will I cook?"

Andie dashed from the car and burst into the house. Bev was sprawled on the couch listening to Joni Mitchell and brushing a euphoric-looking kitty lang. "What's gotten into you, woman?" she asked.

Andie was out of breath from running. "Hon, you're never going to believe this. Dr. Nina Dupree is a dyke!"

Chapter 6

The Mountain Women's Outreach Center was located in an old storefront building on a side street downtown. Bev looked at the window display, a still life with a handmade quilt, a churn, and a dulcimer. Painted on the window were the words *The Mountain Women's Outreach Center — Family, Community, Sisterhood.* It was a nice motto.

Bev checked her reflection quickly in the window, making sure her blouse was tucked into her skirt. Whenever she dressed up, her clothes had a way of becoming immediately disheveled, as if her body were rebelling against the very idea of dressing for success. When she walked in the door, she was immediately bombarded by the enthusiasm of a young blonde woman whom she assumed was Michelle.

"There you are! You must be Beverly; it's so nice to meet you!"

Bev extended her hand in what she hoped was a professional handshake. She noticed with some relief that the young woman was wearing jeans and tennis shoes. Good. Tomorrow she would dress down. "It's nice to meet you, too — Michelle?"

Michelle smiled and rolled her eyes self-deprecatingly. "Ditsy me — saying it's nice to meet you and then not saying who I am. Yes, I'm Michelle."

"I thought I recognized your voice from the phone." It was a distinctive voice, chipper and squeaky, with a slight Appalachian twang.

"Well, Beverly, I thought the first thing we'd do is go on a tour of the center, so you'll know where everything is."

"Sounds good."

Michelle stretched out her arms to indicate the large room they were standing in. "This is our thrift store." There were racks of women's, men's, and children's clothing and a few shelves of used housewares. "Shipments of clothing come in the first Wednesday of every month at seven in the morning. We all come in early to help sort out the clothes." She grinned apologetically. "See, I've already given you something to look forward to."

"Give me an IV drip of coffee, and I'll be fine."

Michelle giggled. "We also take clothing donations from the community, but those are few and far between. There are more people in need here than there are people who can afford to give." She gestured to a corner of the room where two battered sofas sat. A coffeemaker, plastic foam cups, and baskets of nondairy creamer and sugar sat on a table under a sign that read Kaffeeklatsch Korner. "Speaking of coffee, this is our hospitality corner over here. We always keep coffee made, and we have a few women who come here to kind of take a coffee break from their home life."

She led Bev out of the main room and down a narrow hallway. "On the left is our little classroom." The room truly was little and was furnished with cast-off school desks. "This is where we have our GED classes and our mothers' nutrition and childcare classes." She gestured toward the end of the hall. "Back there's just storage space, not much to see. The little girls' room is back there, too."

"Always good to know." The little girls' room. That's what Bev's mother had always said, too. She bet Michelle called peeing *tinkling*.

"And on the right is our office." Michelle led her into a room with three desks. One of the desks was occupied by a woman with long, gray, frizzy hair. A sign on her desk read Teresa Malone, Program Director.

The woman looked up from her work and smiled broadly. "Is this Beverly?"

Bev wasn't sure if she were supposed to answer or let Michelle answer for her. "Yes," Michelle said, settling the issue. "Beverly Jennings, Teresa Malone."

Teresa hopped up from behind her desk and grasped both of Bev's hands in hers. "Beverly, I can't tell you how excited we are to have you here.

Michelle told me about all the work you've done with women's issues, and I just can't imagine that there's a more qualified woman for this position."

"Thank you," Bev said, relieved that Teresa had finally let go of her hands. Teresa's accent was crisp, not from Kentucky — Michigan maybe. "I feel kind of silly asking you this, but what exactly is my position?"

"Sit, sit, and we'll talk about it. Why don't we pull our chairs in a circle? I don't like talking to someone from behind a desk; it really cuts people off from one another, don't you think?"

Bev and Michelle pulled chairs over and sat in front of Teresa like kindergartners gathering around their teacher for story time. "Now," Teresa began, the tone of her voice doing nothing to dispel the kindergarten image, "Michelle is the business manager, just like the sign on her desk says." Bev glanced over at Michelle's desk. In addition to the sign, there was a miniature teddy bear in a pink lace dress and a needlepoint sampler that read, "I will lift up mine eyes unto the hills from whence cometh my help." Teresa's desk was a much more spartan affair; the items that covered it were necessary and meticulously arranged. "And I am the program director," Teresa continued, "which makes you, Beverly, the education coordinator."

"That sounds good —" Bev began.

"It does, doesn't it?" Teresa interrupted. "Titles are real self-esteem boosters, aren't they?"

"They certainly are," Bev said. While the center seemed like a worthwhile place to work, the perkiness factor was going to take some getting used to. "And what will my duties be?"

"Well," Michelle said, "the girl who was here before —"

"Michelle," chided Teresa.

Michelle repeated the self-deprecating grin-eye roll that Bev had seen earlier. "Sorry. The *woman* who was here before taught our mothers' nutrition and childcare class. We thought you could take that over."

"I suppose I could," Bev said, thinking of how the public speaking class she had taken in college had filled her with terror. She had never taught before, had never even considered teaching. Still, she was fairly familiar with the subject matter.

"Are you a mother, Beverly?" Teresa asked, beaming.

"No, but I did grow up with four younger brothers and sisters, so I've changed my share of diapers."

"That's good."

"I've worked in family planning for years, and I minored in health in college."

"Wonderful," Teresa said. "It sounds like you're our new nutrition and childcare teacher."

"You'll have other duties as education coordinator, too," Michelle said. "You won't teach the GED class — we have a woman from Randall who comes over and does that — but you will be in charge of advertising both the GED and the nutrition and childcare courses. You can make flyers, call the radio station, put announcements in the paper, that kind of thing."

"That sounds manageable. How often does this class I'll be teaching meet?"

"There are twelve hour-long classes, once a week," Teresa said.

"Okay, but if you don't mind my saying, so far this doesn't exactly sound like a full-time job."

"You'll have other duties, too," Teresa said. "We all do grunt work here; we don't have any choice since we're a three-person operation. Besides, I always say a little grunt work is good for the soul."

"We thought you could run the cash register in the thrift store during the day, make sure there's coffee, stuff like that," Michelle said.

"It's been a while since I've run a cash register, but I'll give it a try." Bev actually wasn't bothered by the idea of minding shop during the day. Since she was somewhat daunted by the idea of teaching the class, she was glad the rest of her job was going to be fairly low-pressure.

Teresa glanced at her watch and became as frantic as the White Rabbit in *Alice in Wonderland*. "Goodness me, it's time for us to open! Beverly, do you have any quick questions?"

"None that I can think of."

"Michelle and I are delighted to have you here, and we certainly want you to come to us with your thoughts and suggestions. We're all equals here; we don't want you to feel like the low woman on the totem pole just because you're new here."

"Thanks."

"We've got lots of books on nutrition and childcare if you want to look at them while you work the register," Michelle said. "The shop's usually pretty slow."

Two hours passed. Bev had drunk half a pot of coffee and scanned her way through a book on nutrition during pregnancy, and no one had come into the store. She flipped through a lost-in-the-sixties booklet on natural childbirth and snickered when she discovered that the author insisted on calling the mother's vulva her *pussy willow*. Then, finally, the bell on the door jingled, and a thin, hollow-cheeked woman entered the store and made a beeline for the coffeemaker.

"Good morning," Bev called cheerfully.

The woman jumped as if she had been caught in some wrongdoing. "I thought I'd get me a cup of this coffee if you don't care."

"Help yourself," Bev said. "Come to think of it, I might have some, too." Her nerve endings were already jangling from excessive caffeine, but she was so happy to see someone come into the store she felt like she ought to be sociable. She sat across from the woman in the *Kaffeeklatsch Korner*. Unfortunately, her close presence only seemed to succeed in making the woman more nervous.

"You care if I smoke?" the woman asked, taking a pack of cigarettes out of her vinyl purse with a shaking hand. She had the pale, jittery look of a person who subsisted almost entirely on cigarettes and coffee.

"Not if I can join you," Bev said. "I haven't had a cigarette all morning." This seemed to put the woman more at ease, and they smoked for a moment in silence.

"You ain't been workin' here long, have you?" she finally asked.

"No, this is my first day."

"You tired of it yet?"

"No, not really. Why do you say that?"

"It just don't seem like it'd be that interestin',

that's all. You know, you get some women in here buyin' clothes for their young'uns ever now and again, but other'n that, don't nobody come here for nothin' but the free coffee."

"You are the first person who's come in all day."

"And I might be the last un, too."

"Hmm." Bev took a thoughtful drag on her cigarette. "Why don't more people come here?"

The woman leaned forward and whispered, "Where's that northern woman that runs this place?"

"Teresa? She's back in the office. Has been all morning."

"It's her," the woman said, stubbing out her cigarette. "Don't nobody like her, and I reckon I ain't no diffe'rnt."

Bev was starting to get paranoid. "Is it because she's northern?" she whispered.

"I reckon that's part of it. Course, you're from up north, too. I can tell by the way you talk, but I don't hold it agin' you or nothin'. You can't help it, I reckon. But see, you and her is differnt. Like when I say, 'You care if I smoke?' you say go ahead, and then you sit right down and smoke with me. Now that's how a normal person acts. But if I say 'You care if I smoke?' to her, she says, 'Yes, I do care, but go ahead anyway.' And then she goes to her office and comes back with all these little booklets on how bad it is for you to smoke. Honey, I know how bad it is to smoke 'cause by husband is sittin' in my house right now bad off with the emphysema. I look after him all the time, but my daughter, she comes by to see him of a mornin', and I walk down here, you know, just to get out of the house a spell and drink me a cup of coffee and smoke me a cigarette in peace. So the last thing I need is some woman from up north preachin' me a sermon about smokin'."

"I see what you mean." Bev did see the woman's point; at the same time, she wondered if she would maintain her appetite for nicotine if she lived with someone who was dying of emphysema. "Did you tell Teresa about your husband?"

"Honey, she don't listen. That woman loves to hear herself talk better'n anybody I ever seen. She thinks what we need around here is to learn how to macramé and square dance and make Christmas decorations out of bread dough. That woman already has her mind made up; there ain't no need to bother her with the truth."

"I think the nutrition and childcare class here is a pretty good idea." Bev hoped that the woman would affirm that what she was doing was at least worthwhile. "I'm going to be teaching it."

"You're teachin' it, huh? Well, I might tell my granddaughter to take it then. She's fixin' to make me a great-grandmother."

"A great-grandmother. Wow. If you don't mind my asking, how old are you?" It was impossible to tell; she looked haggard but not particularly ancient.

"I'm fifty-two years old." She drained her coffee cup. "Well, I reckon I orta be headin' back; it's gettin' to be about Joe's dinner time."

"It was nice talking to you."

"Well," she said, getting up to leave.

Bev had never heard the word *well* spoken that way — not as an introduction to some other phrase, but as a simple declarative sentence. She watched the woman as she opened the door, then remembered that she had never gotten around to introducing herself. “I’m Bev, by the way,” she called.

The woman turned around to face her. “I’m Wanda.”

Bev watched her first and last customer of the day walk up the side street until she was out of sight.

Chapter 7

As Andie covered the fudge mocha cake in plastic wrap, kitty lang rubbed against her ankles, meowing plaintively. "Have you fed the cat yet, hon?" Andie called. "She's acting like she's starving."

"She's a lying bitch then," Bev said, walking into the kitchen. "I fed her not fifteen minutes ago. Do I look okay in this?"

Andie surveyed her lover, dapper in a white tuxedo-style blouse and black pants. "You look gorgeous, hon."

Bev was suddenly behind her with her arms around her. "So do you."

Andie felt Bev pull her hair back to plant a kiss on her neck. "Now, sweetie, we can't get distracted. Nina and Inez are expecting us."

Bev mumbled into her neck, "But I like getting distracted. Besides, if Nina and Inez have been together thirty-two years, I'm sure they've been late for a few dinner engagements in their time."

Andie pulled herself away gently. "Maybe so, but this is our first social engagement as a couple since we moved here, and I want it to go off without a hitch."

"All right, all right. We'll get there on time like good girls. But you have to carry the cake."

Nina and Inez's house was a cozy little brick cottage built sometime in the thirties. The lawn was perfectly manicured, and the flower beds were bursting with pansies and snapdragons.

Nina answered the door dressed in an emerald green shirtwaist dress and her hair rolled in pink plastic curlers that were only partially hidden beneath a flowered scarf. Her hands flew up to pat the scarf self-consciously. "Goodness gracious, y'all are both heah, and I've still got cuhlers in my haih! I'm just so embarrassed I don't know what to do. I lost track of the time, what with one thing and anothuh. Why, you must be Bevuhly."

"Nice to meet you —"

"Y'all come in, come in. Why, Andrea, that's a lovely frock yoah wearin', and this cake you brought looks delicious. Heah, let me take it. Inez, the gulls ah heah! Inez!"

The living room looked remarkably similar to Nina's office: Victorian chairs, camelback sofa, floral prints. Inez came swaggering down the hallway wearing a Randall College Lady Jaguars sweatshirt and athletic shorts. Her legs were muscular.

"I want you to look at huh," Nina exclaimed. "I told huh to put on somethin' nice, and she comes out in those same ol' shohts she always weahs around the house."

"You look comfortable," Andie said.

"Thank you. I'm Inez." Her voice was as southern-accented as Nina's but at least half an octave deeper.

"Inez," Nina said, handing her the cake. "This is Andrea and Bevuhly. Why don't you take this lovely cake to the kitchen and get ouh guests somethin' to drink. I simply must go and get these cuhlers out of my haih!" She turned to Andie and Bev. "Gulls, please sit. Get comfy."

Nina scurried down the hallway, and Inez disappeared into the kitchen while Andie and Bev settled into matching Victorian chairs. When Andie was sure that neither Nina nor Inez could see them, she turned to Bev and mouthed, "Aren't they cute?" Bev smiled and nodded.

Inez returned with a silver tray holding a decanter of sherry and four glasses. "I hope you ladies like sherry."

"I love it," Andie said. Actually, she preferred beer, but this was obviously going to be a genteel evening, and a genteel evening called for a genteel beverage.

Nina swept into the room with her hair perfectly

coiffed and a fresh coat of lipstick applied. "Well, my wuhd, Inez. I hope you asked these gulls if it was all right for us to suhve alcohol. What with Randall bein' a no-alcohol campus and this bein' a dry county — why, these gulls just might take a dim view of us."

"Nina, it's fine," Inez said.

"It really is," Bev added. "Andie and I both drink socially."

"Well, of coahse you do," Nina said, seeming much relieved. "You ah sophisticated gulls from the big city. I was just fohgettin' myself. So many people 'round heah ah teetotaluhs, and you can't be too careful."

"It's true," Inez said. "You know theah ah people at Randall who would find fault with me for bein' dean of women if they knew I had a sherry befoah dinner or a glass of beah on a hot day."

"Yes," Nina added, starting to talk the exact second Inez had finished. "You and I ah so lucky, Andrea. The people in the English depahtment ah moah relaxed about that soht of thing. I know Payne has a cocktail every now and then, and Bobby buys sherry foah us when he goes up to Lexington."

"Now Bobby's a man who likes a beah on a hot day," Inez said.

"Yes," Nina agreed, "And I can recall more than one hot day when you sat out on that back porch with Bobby and had moah than one beah, listenin' to him tell ahmy stories."

"Bobby's a great guy," Andie said. "You need to meet him, Bev."

"Oh, Bobba's just wondaful," Nina said,

pronouncing Bobby as though it ended with an *a* instead of a *y*. "Of coahse, I nevuh can figure why you like his ahmy stories so much."

"I always thought it would be fun to be in the ahmy," Inez said. "My brothuh was, you know, and I used to have the best time when I was a young gull puttin' on his unifohm and mahchin' around. Of coahse, when Nina and I were growin' up, gulls didn't go 'round doin' things like joinin' the ahmy. You could be a Wac or a Wave of coahse, but they wuh just glorified secretaries. Boys got to do all the fun stuff. You gulls now ah so lucky; you have so many options."

"Well," said Nina, "I suppose I should go get suppuh on the table. Inez, you stay right wheah you ah and entahtain the gulls. We don't want any broken dishes tonight. Bevuhly, Inez is simply a terrah in the kitchen. She makes me so nuhvous I just do everything myself."

"Listen to huh, makin' it sound like I don't uhn my keep," Inez said. "Ovah the yeahs, Nina and I have luhned that there are just some things it's best if I do and some things it's best if she does. Like mowin' the lawn. It's best if I do that because —"

"Don't tell that story," Nina giggled.

"Because several years ago when we fuhst bought a ridin' lawnmowah, Nina said, 'Oh, I want to try it, I want to try it.' So finally I said, 'Well, go ahead then.' And the next thing I know, she's run the thing up a tree and wrecked it. Now how, I ask you, Andrea, do you run a ridin' lawnmowah up a tree?"

"I was just drivin' along thinkin' about Jane Austen," Nina said, "and the next thing I knew I was lyin' on my side with the lawnmowah right on top of me. Why, it's a wonduh I didn't positively maim myself!"

"It certainly is," Bev said, laughing.

"Well, I want you to listen to us," Nina said. "I bet these gulls must think we'ah just terrible, but we do love to tell stories on each othuh!"

When Andie and Bev and Inez were called into the dining room, the table was covered with an impressive spread: roast beef, mashed potatoes, gravy, green beans, creamed corn, yeast biscuits, and a huge pitcher of iced tea.

"Why, Nina, this looks just wonderful," Andie said. "You shouldn't have gone to all this trouble."

"It wasn't any trouble at all. I love to cook for friends. I just hope it's fit to eat."

The meal surpassed being simply fit to eat. Between bites, Bev said, "So, Inez, Andie tells me you're the dean of women. What exactly does that job entail?"

"Well, unfohtunately, a lot of it involves disciplinin' ouwa more recalcitrant female students. Of coahse, it's not so hahsh a task as it used to be. Did you know that at Randall in the sixties the dean of women had to measure gulls' skuht lengths to make sure they wuhn't exposin' too much leg?"

"And up until the early seventies, the gulls had to wear skuhts or dresses — no slacks allowed," Nina added.

"I wouldn't have lasted long under those rules," Bev said.

Inez laughed. "Neithah would I. Fahtunately, during that time I was still teachin' PE, so I was allowed to dress comf'tably."

"I always tell Inez that the only reason she

majahed in physical education was so she didn't have to teach in dresses and high heels."

"But back to your question, Bevuhly," Inez continued. "While the job may not require the strictness it did in the fifties, gulls today can think up ways to misbehave that gulls in the fifties would never have dreamed about. Boys in theah rooms all houhs of the night, smokin' mauhjuana . . ." She trailed off, shaking her head and humming, "Hm, hm, hm."

"Yeah, I guess young women today are more creative," Andie said, thinking that there were probably plenty of female students in the fifties who sneaked boys into their dorm rooms. Of course, why should that occur to Inez? Sneaking boys into her private quarters had surely never been a temptation.

"We had a pahticulahly difficult case last yeah," Inez was saying.

"Inez, I don't know if you should be talkin' about this —"

"Nina, we'ah all grown gulls here." Inez took a sip of tea and continued. "One of our resident assistants came to me, and she was positively in teahs, she was so embahrassed. It seems that she had been knockin' on this gull's doah to check huh room for room inspection, you know. And the gull wasn't answerin' huh doah, even though the resident assistant knew she was in theah. So on a whim, she tried the doah and opened it to find the gull in bed *naked* with anothah gull! She was just so embahrassed she didn't know what to do, so natuhally she tuhned in theah names to me."

"And what did you do?" Andie asked, not sure where this was going.

"Well, I called those gulls into my office, and I explained to them that they wuh engagin' in behaviah that was not fittin' to young Christian ladies. Natuhally, they had to be dismissed from school. I felt a little sahry for them, you know, because theah sickness wasn't really theah fault, but I saw no choice in the mattuh. I mean, they wuh lesbians."

Bev looked as though she had been hit with a ball-peen hammer. "You're kidding, right?"

Inez shook her head gravely. "Oh, Bevuhly, I wish I wuh, but it's true. They wuh lesbians. I mean, can you imagine — grown gulls like that stickin' theah finguhs in each othuh!"

Nina set her iced tea glass down hard. "Inez, I think we've heahd enough. Why, I can tell from the looks on theah faces that you've shocked poah Andrea and Bevuhly half to death. You must fahgive Inez; she does go on sometimes. Now, Andrea, I think it's about time that we cut that lovely cake of yoahs."

Andie was shocked, as shocked as she had ever been in her life, but not for the reasons Nina thought. Thank God the two of them talked so much that they hadn't given her a chance to say anything revealing about her and Bev's relationship. "May I be excused to go to your bathroom?" she asked. She needed to be alone for a minute to pull herself together.

"Why, of coahse, deah. It's down at the end of the hall on the right."

As Andie made her way to the bathroom, she heard Nina's voice in the dining room saying, "Well, I hope you'ah happy, Inez. You've made the poah gull positively ill."

Andie sat on the toilet minutes after she had stopped peeing. She glanced at the magazine rack and saw copies of *Good Housekeeping* and *Sports Illustrated*. No need to look at the address labels to determine which belonged to whom. It made enough sense if they were dykes. But if they weren't, it was just too weird to think about. A piece of cake, a cup of coffee, then she and Bev would make their exit as quickly as possible.

On her way back down the hall, Andie peeked into the house's two bedrooms. One had a white French provincial bedroom suite with a frilly yellow bedspread and matching curtains. The other had a plain wooden captain's bed with a navy bedspread and a bedside lamp the base of which was a blue-and-white University of Kentucky basketball.

In the car on the way home, Bev lit a cigarette and said, "I'll tell you, honey, I don't think I've ever spent a weirder evening."

Andie was still having a difficult time processing the information she had been inadvertently given. "They're . . . not . . . dykes."

Bev heaved an exasperated sigh. "Of course they are. They're just acting like they're not. If everybody thinks they're just a couple of old maid schoolteachers, then nobody will give them any trouble."

Andie pulled the car into the driveway. "No, you're wrong, Bev. They are just a couple of old maid schoolteachers. If they aren't, then why would they be so openly homophobic around us?" Andie looked down at her key ring, trying to remember which key was the house key.

"Because," Bev said, "they didn't want us making any dangerous assumptions."

Andie turned the key in the door. "Honestly, Bev, I hardly think those two old ladies would be so cloak-and-dagger." She flopped on the couch. "My God, they have separate rooms that look like the girls' room and the boys' room on the fucking *Brady Bunch*."

Bev sat down in the chair, making Andie wonder if she were sitting far away from her on purpose. "Your point being?"

"My point being that they have separate rooms, and they say they're not dykes. Sometimes you just have to take things at face value."

Bev leapt up out of her chair and stalked over to face Andie. "Okay, fine, then. By that definition, we're not dykes either."

"What do you mean?"

"You don't say you're a dyke, and when we moved here you insisted we set up that other bedroom. So by that definition, we're not dykes either."

"Bev, that's absurd."

"You're damn right it's absurd. I remember a time when we used to openly share a one-bedroom apartment and have dinner with real dyke friends who didn't talk about 'gulls stickin theah finguhs in each othuh.' "

"It always comes down to my taking this job, doesn't it?"

"No, it always comes down to the way you took this job. Well, goddamn it, you may not be a dyke anymore, but I sure as hell am." Bev ran to the front door and yanked it open. "Hey, everybody," she screamed. "I'm a dyke! I'm a fucking dyke!"

Andie jumped up and slammed the door shut. She

was trying not to cry. That's the way it always was when they fought. Bev yelled, and Andie cried. Of course, they used to just fight over little things. It never used to be like this. "Bev, stop, please."

"Why? Because people might hear? Because you're ashamed to be with me? Look, I'm just really fucking sick of this. You wanted that futon in the front bedroom so bad, then fine. Sleep on it." Bev ran to the back bedroom and slammed the door. Andie sank down in the nearest chair. Now the tears came for real.

Chapter 8

"Sugar, I could've told you about Inez Ratliff and Nina Dupree," Cricket said, nibbling on his chicken salad sandwich. "Y'all aren't the first people to make that little old mistake, believe you me."

"Oh, yeah?" Bev and Cricket were sitting at the Queen Anne dining table in Cricket's apartment. After the blowup on Friday night, Bev had called Cricket just to have someone to talk to. In Boston, she would've called a girlfriend, but in Morgan, Cricket was the closest thing to a girlfriend that she had. He had invited her to come to lunch on

Monday, and now she sat in his gorgeous, antique-filled apartment — gorgeous if you got over the fact that it occupied the floor just above the funeral home.

"Honey, that one semester I spent at Randall I just had the hardest time. You know, people go there from all over, not just from Morgan, so none of 'em gave two shits if I was a Needham or not. To them I was just some little faggot to make fun of or beat up. The jocks were the worst. You know how them Christian athletes are; they think they can beat you into loving the Lord. I was just as miserable as I could be. But I had Dr. Dupree for freshman English, and I really liked her. I knew she lived with Dr. Ratliff — everybody knows about her and Dr. Ratliff — and so I decided I'd go talk to her about my little problem."

"Bad idea."

"The worst, honey. I marched into her little office, and I told her I didn't know what to do because a lot of people were givin' me a hard time 'cause I was gay. And she says, 'You're what?' And I say, 'I'm gay — you know, homosexual.' And she says — you know how she talks — she says, 'Oh, Cricket, that's simply hahrible. What a tragic life you must lead. Have you evah considahed seekin' medical help foah yoah unfohtunate illness?' And of course, I knew about her and Inez, so —"

"You thought she was kidding."

"Exactly. But she kept on talkin' 'til I knew she was just as serious as a heart attack. Honey, that's when I finally said fuck it and decided to go off to

Lexington to mortician's school like my daddy wanted me to in the first place."

"Wow," Bev said, disturbed that it was homophobia that made Cricket turn to his rather ghoulish line of work.

"Well, you didn't come to listen to me rattle, did you, sugar? You came for some lunch-break therapy, and honey, the doctor is in. So, tell me, did y'all patch things up after your little spat?"

Bev pushed her plate away. "I told you I told her to sleep in the other room."

"Uh-huh."

"I was in that big bed all by myself — the cat wouldn't even get in with me. And I couldn't even think about going to sleep. The longer I lay there, the less angry and the more sad and guilty-feeling I got. I kept thinking that all Andie wants is this job to get her career on track, and I have to be such a bitch about it all the time. So finally, about three-thirty, I tiptoed into the office room and got on the futon next to her. She was asleep, but she rolled over and kind of snuggled up next to me. Later, I made her breakfast and brought it to her in bed, with a little card on the tray that said 'I'm sorry.' "

"That's sweet."

"It seemed to make things okay, for the time being. But the thing is, I know this problem is going to keep coming up. And even if it's shallow of me, as long as she makes a point of keeping our relationship a secret, I'm going to feel like she's ashamed of me." Bev felt a catch in her throat and took a big gulp of tea to wash it down.

Cricket reached across the table and patted her hand. "I know, sugar, but it's not you she's ashamed of. I know it's hard. Hell, it's hard enough just to be gay all by yourself in this town; havin' a gay relationship is damn near impossible."

"Don't say that."

"I said near impossible."

"Well, that's a big comfort. The thing is, too, we can't have friends like we used to — friends that we're honest with. After I first met you, I told Andie you were gay, and the first thing she said was 'You didn't tell him about us, did you?' "

"And what did you say?"

Bev stared at the crumbs on her plate. "I told her no."

"So she thinks I think —"

"That we're cousins."

Cricket retrieved a cut-glass ashtray from the sideboard and lit a cigarette. "Well, that's not a bit awkward, is it?"

"I'm sorry, Cricket. I'm such a hypocrite. I think she's ashamed of me because she keeps our relationship a secret, so then I choose to be open about it with you, and when she asks me about it, I lie. God, sometimes I wonder how far I'd go to keep that woman from being mad at me." Bev lit a cigarette and sighed. "And now you're mad at me."

"Oh lord, hon, I'm not mad at you. These things get complicated, and I don't blame Andie. How's she to know that I wouldn't go off and blab everything I know to my mamaw?"

"I thought small-town life was supposed to be uncomplicated."

“It is, hon, but only if you’re exactly like everybody else.”

Bev smiled. “I guess so. Well, I should be getting back to work. Tonight’s the first meeting of my class, and as Nina Dupree would say, ‘I’m just so nuhvous. Ah just don’t know what to do!’ ”

Cricket laughed. “Thanks for comin’ over.”

“Thanks for having me . . . and feeding me . . . and therapizing me. I feel like I should write you a check or something.”

“Money I’ve got. I’m just happy to have a new girlfriend to talk to.”

Bev flashed a sly grin. “Wait ’til Mamaw Needham hears I’m your new girlfriend.”

“Oh lord, hon, that old biddy’ll be plannin’ our weddin’!” He rose from his chair. “Here, let me walk you downstairs. I don’t like makin’ a friend walk through the funeral home all by herself. It’s kinda creepy if you’re not used to it.”

In the hallway downstairs, past the door marked Dangerous — Employees Only, hung a huge lighted painting of a blond-haired, blue-eyed Jesus. Bev couldn’t help but stare at the strangely WASPish deity. “Aren’t funeral homes supposed to be secular? Might you not offend people by having this picture up here?”

Cricket patted her shoulder affectionately. “Hon, this is the Bible Belt. Far more people’d be offended if we didn’t have one of these awful things hangin’ up.” He pecked Bev on the cheek. “Good luck with your class tonight, sugar.”

* * * * *

"I need to check my bag to make sure I've got all my papers." Bev rushed frantically across the living room, nearly tripping over kitty lang.

"Hon, they were all there when you looked two minutes ago. I seriously doubt that any of them have gone anywhere," Andie said.

"I'm sorry; I'm nervous."

"It's kind of cute. I'm sure you remember what a basket case I was the first time I had to teach. I was so scared I had to pretend I was Maggie Smith in *The Prime of Miss Jean Brodie* just to make myself able to speak in front of all those people. It was all I could do not to talk with a Scottish accent."

"And who am I supposed to pretend to be?"

"Sidney Poitier in *To Sir, With Love*?" She took Bev's face in her hands. "You'll do fine, hon. Just remember as you walk into that classroom that you're in control. Before you know it, the old adrenaline will have kicked in, and you'll be perfectly at ease."

Bev kept repeating *I'm in control, I'm in control* in her mind as she prepared to walk into the classroom at the Mountain Women's Outreach Center. But when she did enter, instead of seeing a sea of unfamiliar faces, there were only two faces. One of them belonged to Wanda.

"I brung my granddaughter like I said I would," she said. "Bev, this here is Tammy."

Tammy was a pretty blonde teenager wearing a black T-shirt with the face of some cowboy-hat-wearing country-and-western singer on it. Her eyes were huge and innocent.

"Nice to meet you, Tammy," Bev said.

“Nice to meet you, too,” Tammy whispered, casting her eyes downward.

“This ’un here’s like my own young’un,” Wanda said, nodding affectionately in Tammy’s direction. “Her mama left her for me to raise, and now I reckon we’ve got another littl’un comin’ on. Tell the lady what you’re gonna name the baby, Tammy.”

Tammy patted her tummy self-consciously. It hadn’t even started to bulge yet. “Britanny if it’s a girl, Morgan if it’s a boy.”

“You can tell she likes them stories on the TV,” Wanda said. “Them people’s got the craziest names.”

Bev assumed that Wanda was talking about soap operas. “They sure do,” she said. “So, Tammy, how old are you?”

“Seventeen.”

“She’s a senior over at the high school,” Wanda said. “Just ’cause she’s pregnant ain’t no reason for her to quit school. I quit school to have my first baby, and I’ve always wished I hadn’t. Quit school, I mean. She’s due in March. If we’re lucky, she’ll have it over the spring break. If we ain’t lucky, well, I reckon she can take a week off and then go back and finish. I can take care of it ’til she’s through. Takin’ care of babies is second nature to me. Mom had so many of ’em I reckon I’ve had me a young’un on my hip since I was eight year old.”

“I know how that goes,” Bev said. “I have four younger brothers and sisters.”

“Yeah?” Wanda said. “I had six. Course, two of ’em’s dead now.”

As they were talking, another woman walked in. She appeared to be in her late thirties.

“Hey,” Wanda said to the new woman. “Ain’t you Jack Barnes’s girl?”

“Yeah,” she said, “I’m Charlene Peters, used to be Charlene Barnes.”

“Have a seat, Charlene. I’m Bev. I’m going to be teaching this class.”

Charlene squinted at her suspiciously. “Well, honey, I don’t reckon there’s much you can teach me. This here’s my fourth baby, but my social worker said I orta be here, so here I am.” She plopped down resentfully in the nearest seat.

“Bev, you don’t care if I stay for this class, do you?” Wanda asked. “I know I ain’t pregnant nor nothin’, but I do do all the cookin’ for Tammy, so I figgered I might could learn somethin’ about what she orta be eatin’.”

“Of course you can stay,” Bev said, touched that Wanda was concerned for her granddaughter and future great-grandchild’s health.

A young girl crept shyly into the classroom. Red-haired and freckle-faced, she looked like she had accidentally wandered into the wrong place while looking for a room where auditions for *Annie* were being held. “Is this the class for, uh, mothers?” she asked, obviously embarrassed.

“Yes. I’m Bev, the teacher.” Bev noted that she needed to make a special effort not to sound condescending; this girl was so young.

“I’m Jeanie,” the girl mumbled.

At seven on the dot, one more student walked in, a tall, strikingly pretty young African-American woman. Like so many tall women, she tried to disguise her height by slouching. She slipped wordlessly to the back of the classroom and sat down.

"Hi, I'm Bev. I'll be teaching this class." She waited for the young woman to respond, before prompting her with, "And you are?"

"Huh?" she said. "Oh. Lisa."

The topic that night was nutrition during pregnancy. Bev handed out charts showing how many servings from the different food groups a pregnant woman should eat each day. She discussed healthy ways to satisfy food cravings and handed out recipes for snacks. Talking to the class wasn't as intimidating as she thought it would be, particularly since there were only five people present.

The problem was that only Tammy and Wanda seemed interested in what she was saying. Wanda asked questions about preparing high-iron meals for Tammy, and though Tammy was silent, she looked directly at Bev throughout the class, nodding to show that she was paying attention.

The other women didn't fare so well. Charlene stared into space and periodically heaved blatantly bored sighs. Jeanie hunched down in her seat and didn't look up. She seemed embarrassed by everything having to do with pregnancy — even a subject as mundane as nutrition. Fifteen minutes into class, Lisa took out a nail file and began giving herself a manicure. By the time class was over, Bev could see that her teaching methods, which she had had all of one hour to develop, already needed major revision.

When she got home, Andie met her at the door. Bev leaned forward to kiss her hello, but Andie quickly stepped back, saying, "Why, Bev, you're just in time for coffee with Mamaw Needham and me." Bev didn't need a decoder ring to figure out what Andie was saying: Careful, hon, Mamaw Needham has invited herself over for coffee.

"Hidy, Beverly," Mamaw Needham said when Bev walked in. Mamaw was slurping coffee and petting kitty lang, who was settled blissfully in her soft lap. "Cricket told me you come over and had dinner with him today."

"Yeah," Bev said, flopping into the nearest chair.

"Did he cook for you?" Mamaw Needham asked.

"We had chicken salad sandwiches and fruit cups."

"Well, I reckon he was havin' a busy day and so didn't have time to go all out for you. That boy can cook — you never seen the beat! Most fellers don't know their way 'round a kitchen worth a plugged nickel. But Cricket, he's just as handy as he can be. He sure don't get that from his daddy or his papaw. Why, hit's just the quarest thing I've ever seen!"

"Well, the chicken salad and fruit cup were very good," Bev said. Cricket was right. The old woman just didn't have the frame of reference that would make it possible for her to catch a clue.

"How did class go?" Andie asked.

"It wasn't as scary as I thought it would be. Only five women were there, one of whom was the grandmother of one of the students. It wasn't like I was really doing public speaking or anything."

"I bet most of them girls ain't married," Mamaw Needham said after taking a loud slurp of coffee.

"I didn't ask. I didn't figure it was any of my business unless they wanted to tell me. Most of them are awfully young, though. One girl doesn't look any older than fifteen. She just seems so unhappy and . . . embarrassed by it all."

"Bless her heart," Mamaw Needham said, shaking her head. "When I was fifteen I didn't even know where babies come from. I was still lookin' for 'em in under cabbage leafs. But these girls now, they get in over their head way too young. Course, hit's the boys that gets 'em that way; seems like everbody forgets about that. I bet that boy who got that little girl in trouble is down at the pool hall actin' foolish while she sits in your class tryin' to figger out what to do with her life."

"Probably so," Bev said.

"Well, girls, I reckon I better be takin' off. Ancil's gonna be in the bed a-wonderin' where I'm at — to go to sleep, I mean!" She cackled. "I remember that babies don't come from in under cabbage leafs, but in the past thirty years or so, I've about forgot where they do come from!"

Andie laughed. "You take care of yourself, Mamaw Needham."

"You, too, honey," she said. She patted Bev on the shoulder on her way out. "And Beverly, you take good care of my grandson."

After Mamaw Needham had safely waddled away, Bev slumped back in her chair, exhausted. "Whew!" she sighed.

Andie stood behind her and massaged her shoulders. "How're you feeling, hon?"

Bev looked up at her and smiled ruefully. "Like a visitor to another planet."

Chapter 9

Andie was beginning to wonder if Gary Clark from the history department were flirting with her. She was generally oblivious to men's advances, in the same way she was oblivious to football games on television and other things that held no interest for her, but lately she noticed that Gary seemed to make a point of being in the same place as she. This morning she had been at the coffeemaker listening to Payne Symington hold forth on his favorite (and, as far as Andie knew, only) topic of conversation: his southern boyhood.

Payne, Andie had recently learned through Bobby, was the author of several unpublished and apparently unpublishable novels on the subject of poor-but-sensitive southern boys coming of age. His only work in print, a novella titled *My New Kentucky Home*, had been published by Randall College Press. Of course, Randall didn't really have a press; they simply had run the pages off on a copying machine, printed up some covers on heavy paper, and then stapled the things together. The novella, surprisingly enough, dealt with a poor-but-sensitive southern boy who came to Randall College on a scholarship in the twenties. Randall had held a book-signing party and had given numerous copies to donors.

Bobby had a copy of *My New Kentucky Home* in his office and had let Andie look at it. She had scanned the first page, on which the narrator described the tear-stained face of his mother upon his departure for college, and the last page, on which the narrator declared that the mountains of Kentucky would always be in his blood. She had smiled, shrugged, and handed the book back to Bobby.

On this particular morning, Payne had been discussing his boyhood habit of skinny-dipping in cow ponds with his friends: "Why, honey, we swam in so many cow ponds growin' up, it's a wonduh the leeches didn't just suck us dry!" Andie had been silently wondering if any other form of sucking had gone on among all those naked boys in the cowponds when Gary had walked in.

"The coffeemaker in the history office is on the fritz," he had said. "Mind if I steal a cup?" After filling his mug, he had instantly turned to Andie. "A student in my Western civ class was just asking me what modernist literature she should read to deepen her understanding of the period. I couldn't help but notice the Virginia Woolf poster in your office, and I was wondering what you might recommend."

Gary had listened with apparent fascination as she held forth on Woolf and Stein and Pound and H.D. He had listened for the entire duration of a cup of coffee, after which he thanked her profusely and excused himself to go teach. She had turned back to Payne to see him smiling at her.

"It's hahd to believe that Gary is now the most eligible bacheluh on campus," he had said. "Why, it only seems like yestuhday that he was a freckle-faced little tyke who used to come to my office and beg for candy."

"What do you mean?"

"Honey, Gary was practically raised on this campus. His mama is the directuh of admissions, and his daddy is the academic dean."

"Dean Clark is Gary's dad?"

"That's right." Payne's grin widened. "And you wanna know anothuh secret?"

"What?"

"The coffeemaker in the history depahtment isn't really broken."

"I don't think I follow you."

"What I'm sayin' is that Gary didn't really come in heah for the coffee, and he didn't come in heah to look at my pretty face."

Now, as Andie sat waiting for her office hours to be over, she told herself that what Payne had suggested was ridiculous. She had always believed that intelligent men had a sense of the women who were available to them and the women who were not, and the message she gave at work was always one of unavailability. She always dressed modestly, pulling her hair back and wearing sensible suits, flats, and minimal makeup and jewelry. Her demeanor was pleasant but cool. Her public persona was the *I'll-be-friendly-but-keep-your-distance* Dr. Andrea Pritchard. Her private self, the self that could be funny and sexy and loving, had no place at work. Surely there was no way that Gary could be attracted to Andie's dour public persona. After all, keeping those two selves separate had always protected her. At least so far.

Andie jumped when her office door swung open. "Think fast!" a male voice called.

Without thinking at all, she cupped both hands and caught the spherical object that was hurled at her. She looked up at the face in the door. It was Gary, smiling. "An apple for the teacher," he said. "Thanks for helping me out today." He waved good-bye, then shut the door.

Andie looked down at the shiny, red apple and felt strangely like Snow White.

"I've got an idea," Andie said brightly when she got home. "Bobby says there's a steakhouse up the road in Taylorsville that's pretty good. Why don't we go there tonight?"

"Really?" Bev said, obviously thrilled. "Us, out to dinner in public? Just like a real, live couple?"

"Just like a real, live couple," Andie said, "only

no public displays of affection. And if we run into somebody from Randall, I have to introduce you as my cousin."

Bev grinned. "It's a deal, but you know what? I'm going to wear that silk V-neck shirt that drives you absolutely crazy!"

The Wrangler Steakhouse was more elegant than the Dixie Diner. Of course, that wasn't saying much. The lighting was dim, which was fairly romantic, but when the hostess seated Andie and Bev, it was at a table directly under a stuffed deer's head that hung on the wall. When the waitress — a woman wearing more blue eye shadow than seemed physically possible — came to take their order, Bev said, "The lady will have the sirloin, medium well, with baked potato and broccoli on the side. I'll have the rib eye, medium rare, with fries and cole slaw, and," gesturing toward the deer's head, "my friend here wants a green salad, no dressing." The waitress knit her brow at her, then stalked off.

"I don't think she got your little joke," Andie laughed. "It must be customary for the natives of this area to eat a meal with Bambi staring at them." Andie felt good just being out with Bev. No one from Randall was there, and she felt safe in their couplehood — safe enough to let her foot brush Bev's ankle under the table.

"Careful, there," Bev said. "Our furry chaperon here may not take kindly to . . ." She leaned forward and whispered dramatically, "public . . . displays . . . of . . . affection!"

Andie laughed. "So how are the kind-hearted

missionary women at the Mountain Women's Outreach Center?"

"Oh, kindhearted but wrongheaded as usual. You know what Teresa's next big project for the mountain women is?"

"I'm afraid to guess."

"Vegetarian cooking classes."

"You're kidding, right?"

" 'Fraid not. She thinks it would make 'the underprivileged women of Appalachia,' as she so condescendingly likes to call them, more health-conscious. I tried to tell her there was no way she was going to convert the locals into alfalfa-sprout-and-tofu eaters. You should hear Wanda talk about what she eats. To her, a vegetarian meal is a big pot of pinto beans with half a pig cooked in them."

"And what does Michelle think of this idea?"

"She thinks it's just great. Michelle is Teresa's little disciple; whatever Teresa likes, she likes." She sipped her water. "And did anything fascinating happen at your place of employment today, my dear?"

Andie thought about Gary. Should she even bring it up? She turned her head and saw their waitress coming toward them with a tray. "Look, here's our food."

When the waitress set down their food, there were two steaks with their side dishes and one green salad, no dressing. Andie and Bev waited until the waitress was gone to laugh.

"I tell you what," Andie said. "Why don't we split this salad in Bambi's honor, since he's kind of . . . incapacitated."

Bev picked up a piece of lettuce in her fingers and held it up in a toast to the deer's head. "Here's to ya, pal."

When they got back in the car, Bev put her hand on Andie's knee. "That was nice," she said.

Andie squeezed Bev's hand. "So's this."

"You know what I think we should do?" Bev said, grinning mischievously.

"What?"

"I think we should park."

"Bev, the car is parked." She knew what Bev meant, but she was going to make her say it.

"You know what I mean — drive the car out to some remote setting. You can pretend to run out of gas, and I can pretend to be too dippy to look at the gas gauge. And then . . . we can park and make out."

Andie smiled. "So that's what the rustic folk around here do for excitement."

"Are you up for it?"

Andie had never made out in a parked car before, and she was fairly sure Bev hadn't either. They were city girls, city dykes specifically, and in the city, groping your girlfriend in a parked car on a crowded street wasn't exactly a prudent idea. But here in the country . . . "Okay, but only if we can find someplace really isolated."

Bev snorted. "Like that's a problem here. Just start cruising the back roads, girl."

Andie drove the car down winding country road after winding country road, growing more and more impatient to find a spot. The roads were more heavily populated than she would have guessed. Finally, on impulse, she turned down a gravel road that led to a clearing. There was no house at the end of the road, only a dilapidated barn that appeared abandoned.

She smiled over at Bev and put the car in park. "I think we've found our spot." She leaned over for a kiss.

"Hey, no fair necking in the front in the age of bucket seats!" Bev protested. "What do you think, that I wanna use the gear shift as some kind of sex toy? Get in the backseat, you pervert!"

Andie climbed somewhat awkwardly into the back, and Bev followed her, falling right into her lap. They kissed. There was something exciting about making out in the backseat of a car. It might be cliché, but it still felt deliciously naughty, like they were teenagers out past their curfew. Bev undid the buttons on Andie's blouse, and Andie soon felt the softness of her lover's lips against her flesh. "Ooh," she purred, leaning back in the seat and pulling Bev on top of her. A light flashed in Andie's face which gave her a sudden understanding of how animals caught in headlights must feel. "Don't move, Bev," she whispered through clenched teeth.

A face appeared in the window, the craggy, stubbly face of a middle-aged man wearing a green cap emblazoned with the words *John Deere*. He did not look happy. Suddenly every urban legend Andie had ever heard rang true; one sentence kept repeating itself in her head: "And all they found was a bloody hook."

The man rapped on the window with his fist. Andie held Bev against her chest, terrified. She wouldn't dream of opening the door, but she did manage to push the automatic window opener button with her left big toe, opening the window a tiny crack.

"This here's private property!" the man shouted. "You git on home now, missy." He peered into the car window to see the back of Bev's head. "And take your boyfriend with you!"

"Yes, sir. Sorry, sir," Andie managed to say. The man walked off, muttering about sin and fornication.

"Whew!" Andie breathed, buttoning her blouse. "Thank God he didn't really catch on. He would've shot us and buried us in his cow pasture."

"Boyfriend, my ass," Bev grumbled, climbing into the front seat. "Jesus, I'm not *that* butch."

Andie climbed into the driver's seat and adopted a thick Appalachian accent. "Well, I reckon they ain't used ta seein' no short-haired women 'round these here parts, missy." She started the car. "Shall we go home to the safety of our own bed?"

Chapter 10

By the third meeting of the nutrition and childcare class, Bev had entirely abandoned the idea of teaching in the classroom. Something about the atmosphere made the women inattentive and resentful, as if it were just another high school class to be slept through. Now they were meeting in the Kaffeeklatsch Korner, sitting on the couches and sipping decaf. Bev didn't feel as forced into the role of authority figure as she did in the classroom, and the women were more comfortable and animated. Besides, as their bellies grew more and more distended, it would have become increasingly difficult for them to fit into the tiny school desks in the classroom.

The night's topic was labor and delivery. Bev was trying to describe the process as clinically as possible without glossing over the pain factor. There was no danger of glossing things over too much with Charlene present, however.

"Shoot, when I had my first 'un, hit hurt so bad I thought I was gonna split wide open," she was saying. "When my husband took me into the hospital, I was screamin', 'I'm dyin'! I'm dyin'! Help me, Jesus! I'm dyin'!' I thought I was, too. Don't seem like nothin' could hurt that bad without you was dyin'."

The eyes of all the first-time mothers widened in terror. Charlene sat back, enjoying their fear like she was telling a ghost story around a campfire. "Course, hit's always the first time that hurts the worst," she said.

"Is it really that bad, Nanny?" Tammy asked Wanda.

"I never thought havin' babies was that bad. It hurts and everything, but you can't say you don't get somethin' good for all your trouble."

"Humph," Charlene grunted.

"And of course," Bev said, "if you decide that natural childbirth is too much for you, you have lots of options to help control the pain." Bev went on to discuss the newborn's appearance and the tests the doctor or nurse would perform upon the new baby. "They'll check the baby's pigmentation, for one thing. In healthy white babies, the skin color should be pink, though a little blueness in the extremities usually isn't anything to worry about. In African-

American babies, the color of the mucous membranes and the soles of the hands and feet should be pinkish in color." Bev was on automatic pilot when she delivered this part of her lecture, so she was surprised when she learned it had such a positive effect on one of the persons present.

At the end of class, Lisa went up to her, smiling for the first time Bev could remember. "I just wanted you to know," she said, "that was cool what you said."

Bev was confused. "What do you mean, Lisa?"

"When you said what my baby would look like, you know, not just what the white babies would look like."

"Oh." It hadn't occurred to Bev not to discuss babies of different ethnicities; after all, she wasn't teaching this class for the Ku Klux Klan.

"I graduated from Morgan High School, and the health and biology teachers there never said nothin' about black people."

"They just assumed everybody was white because they were?"

"Yeah, or that black people wasn't worth talkin' about. Anyway, that was cool what you done." She smiled shyly and turned to leave. "See you next week."

"You take care of yourself, Lisa." Bev was disturbed to be living in a place where such a tiny gesture of inclusiveness would be so deeply appreciated.

All the students had left but Jeanie. She had sat on the couch staring blankly for several minutes and was only now getting up and putting on her jacket. Bev had noticed during class that she didn't look well. Her fair skin had a dull grayish cast, and she seemed drained and lifeless.

"Jeanie, are you okay? You don't look well."

"I'm all right. I been sick to my stomach a lot is all."

"That's common during the first trimester. Try to eat some saltines whenever you start feeling nauseated. A lot of the time, putting something in your stomach actually helps."

"Lord, sometimes just thinkin' about food makes me sick to my stomach — and I can't hardly stand to smell it. I work down at the drive-in, and sometimes I'll smell them onion rings and get so sick I have to run to the bathroom and throw up. I ain't told 'em I'm pregnant at work yet, so I reckon they wonder what's wrong with me."

"You go to school and work part-time at the drive-in, too? That's a lot of work."

"Nah, I work full-time at the drive-in. I ain't in school."

"How old are you, Jeanie?"

"I turnt sixteen two months ago. That's old enough to drop out."

"Well, it may be, but isn't it important to get your education?"

"Not if I wanna have money to eat. Look, you don't know what my situation is, okay? So maybe you ort not to be so quick to give me advice." She turned to go.

"But Jeanie, I want to know what your situation is. I want to help."

Jeanie regarded Bev with cold eyes. "But you done told me to eat some crackers when I feel sick to my stomach. Now that's helpin', ain't it? See now, you've helped me. You've gone and done your good deed for the day. Now you can go home and get a good night's sleep, knowin' you helped some poor ol' unfortunate girl." She slammed the door behind her.

Suddenly Bev understood why Teresa liked to come up with ideas like classes in vegetarian cooking and holiday decorating with bread dough. It was so much easier than finding out what people needed and really trying to help them.

Chapter 11

The creatures that fluttered in Andie's stomach were far less benign than butterflies. The minute she had come in this morning, Joyce had told her that Dr. Hill wanted to see her in his office. As she walked toward his half-open door, she felt like a school kid who had just been called in to see the principal.

"Ah, Andrea," Hill waffled the moment he spied her. "Won't you, ah, come in and have a seat?"

Unlike Nina's feminine parlor of an office, Hill's work space was filled only with standard office furniture. The books that spilled from the shelves and a photo of his wife and teenaged daughter provided the room's only decoration.

Andie nodded toward the photo. "Your daughter's very pretty."

"Hmm? Ah. Yes. Miranda. Lovely girl. That's a rather, ah, outdated photograph, I'm afraid. She's married now, ah, lives in Bowling Green, is expecting her first, ah, child."

Andie smiled at him. She was still nervous, but it was important to be solicitous. "So you're going to be a grandpa then?"

"Hmm?" Hill paused a moment, ran his tongue over his teeth, then spoke as if the idea had never occurred to him before. "Ah, yes. Yes. I, ah, suppose I am." He stared into space for a moment, giving Andie ample time to worry about why he had asked to see her. Finally, his eyes focused on her. "Ah. Yes. Well. The reason I, ah, called you here is, ah, to offer you an opportunity of sorts."

"An opportunity?"

"Yes. Allow me to explain, as it were. I don't know how much you know about the history of, ah, our school, that it was founded by Eugenia Randall near the, ah, turn of the century."

"I did know that." Andie was quickly discovering that few things were more frustrating than waiting for Dr. Hill to get to the heart of a matter.

"Good, good, then. Ah, well, the school has, ah, recently acquired a box of, ah, Eugenia Randall's papers. The college already owns most of her papers that relate to her work at the, ah, school. But these papers were, ah, owned by a lady in the community who passed away recently, and she, ah, left them to the school. I, ah, don't really know what bearing if any, these papers have on Randall College. No one has, ah, read them yet, but they seem to be, ah, letters, journal entries, the occasional poem."

"They certainly sound interesting."

"I was hoping you'd say that. Didn't you do your dissertation on something involving women's, ah, letters, journal entries, things of that nature?"

"Women's Life Writing. Yes."

"I was, ah, wondering if you might like to have first crack at these papers, as it were. To be, ah, honest, no one else in the history or, ah, English departments seems that interested, and I thought you, ah, might be."

Unread papers were the exact kind of thing that aroused Andie's curiosity. She loved rifling through boxes of yellowed papers, acting as a private eye whose job it was to piece together a long-dead woman's life. "Dr. Hill, I would be very interested."

"Splendid. You're welcome to do any sort of writing on this subject that you, ah, choose. It's all yours, as it were. But I was, ah, wondering if you would be willing to make a, ah, presentation of sorts to faculty and, ah, students on your findings."

"I'd love to. When?"

"January 10 is Eugenia Randall's, ah, birthday. We at the college usually try to do some, ah, little presentation in honor of that."

"January 10 then."

"Splendid. Of course, if you find that these papers consist of nothing more than the, ah, woman's laundry lists, do let me know, and we, ah, of course, can cancel the whole affair."

For the first time, Andie was one-hundred percent convinced that coming to Randall had been an excellent career move. "It's a deal."

"Marvelous. The, ah, box of papers is currently gathering dust in a basement somewhere on campus. I'll have it sent over to your office this, ah, afternoon."

Andie nearly skipped down the hallway. She was so preoccupied with the excitement of her project that she bumped smack into Gary Clark.

"Oh! Goodness, Gary, I'm sorry. I wasn't paying a bit of attention to where I was going."

He smiled, not seeming at all displeased with the physical contact he had just made with her, however unintentional. "No harm done. As a matter of fact, you were just the woman I was hoping to see."

She unlocked her office door with a slightly shaky hand. "Come in then. Do you need another minilecture on modernism?" She hoped Gary wouldn't notice that the apple he had given her a week ago was still sitting on her desk uneaten.

"I wanted to ask you something," he said sheepishly. "I was wondering, did you get your invitation to Payne's Halloween party?"

"Yes, it's somewhere on my desk." It was a costume party to which all liberal arts faculty were invited. Guests were supposed to go as their favorite literary or historical figure, or some sort of pretentious silliness, Andie remembered.

"Were you planning on going?"

"I thought I would." Andie generally found departmental gatherings awkward, but she felt she had no choice but to go. It suddenly occurred to her. Was Gary about to —

"I was wondering if you'd like to go to the party with me."

Andie forced a pleasant facial expression while her mind reeled in panic. She was a married woman, but she wasn't married in a way she could make Gary or anyone else at Randall understand.

She looked at Gary and tried to decide what she would think of him if she were straight. He wasn't repulsive or anything — thin and bearded with glasses, a pretty standard-looking young male academic type. But she wasn't straight. She loved Bev. And yet if she turned down Gary, son of the academic dean and the director of admissions, it would look suspicious. Besides, two people accompanying each other to a party to which they had each been invited individually didn't really count as a date, did it?

"Yes. I'd like that."

When Andie went to check her mail in the central office that afternoon, Joyce looked up from her *True Confessions* magazine and smiled at her. "I hear you're going to Dr. McAllister's party with Gary Clark." She drew out Gary's name insinuatingly.

"Yes," Andie said, doing her damnedest to sound nonchalant.

"You're going to be the envy of all the single girls at Randall." She nodded over at her mother, who was snoozing away in her customary office chair. "Even mother thinks he's cute."

"Really?" It was all Andie could think of to say. She was beginning to get a feel for how fast news traveled in this small-college, small-town environment. Now everyone thought she and Gary Clark were an item. Shit. What was she going to tell Bev?

Chapter 12

Bev thought Andie was definitely acting funny. All through dinner she had been extra-solicitous of Bev, jumping up to refill her water glass, almost knocking her chair over in her haste to fetch her the pepper. When Bev had told a slightly amusing story about something Teresa had done at work, Andie laughed like it was the funniest damned thing she'd ever heard. And now that they had retired to the living room and were watching an old episode of *The Dick Van Dyke Show* (or "The Penis Van Lesbian Show," as Bev liked to call it), Andie laughed extra loud at the parts Bev seemed to find funny. It was weird. Andie didn't even like the show. Something was wrong. She seemed so eager to please . . . and so jumpy.

Finally Bev could stand it no longer. During a commercial that Andie was pretending to pay a great deal of attention to, Bev turned quickly to her and shouted, "Boo!"

Andie jumped straight off the sofa, her hand flying to her heart. When she sat back down, she said, "Why did you do that?"

"I did it because you're so jumpy you're starting to make *me* nervous." Bev picked up the remote and clicked off the TV. "Is there something you want to talk about?"

"No, I'm fine. It was just kind of a stressful day at work."

"Did something in particular happen that stressed you out?"

"No, no, not really. Just tons of papers to grade, and Hill has a project he wants me to work on. Garden-variety work stress."

The quaver in Andie's voice told Bev that what was bothering her was more than the pressures of academia. "Come on, hon, I've seen you stressed out about school a million times before, and it's never been this bad."

Andie picked at her cuticles nervously. "This is different. I've never had a full-time job before, and it's just so conservative there, I'm always afraid of losing it."

Bev thought she had heard at least a grain of truth. "Did something happen today that made you think you're going to lose your job?"

"Look, I just don't feel like talking anymore. Can't we turn the TV back on?"

"Sure, that way we can sit in the same room and never have to talk to each other or think about our problems. That's the way my family handled things, and you can tell by how often I visit them how well that worked."

"Bev, this is different. I don't want to talk right now, okay? What do you mean 'don't have to think about our problems'? Jesus, what problems?"

Bev felt her jaw clenching. "Oh, that's right. We don't have any problems. Sure, we don't talk like we used to, and we can't have friends like we used to, and about the only thing we do more than we used to is fight. But you're right. We don't have any problems. Our relationship is abso-goddamn-lutely perfect."

"Okay, okay," Andie said, starting to cry. "You wanna know what's bothering me, I'll tell you what's bothering me. There's this guy at work —"

"Oh, Jesus." Bev slumped down with her face in her hands. If the first step in the dissolution of their relationship began with the statement, "We can just tell people we're cousins," then the last step must begin with, "There's this guy at work."

"Bev, are you listening to me?"

"I'm listening." Listening to my life fall apart, Bev thought.

"He's been talking to me a lot lately, and today — well, he asked me to go to a party with him."

"And what did you say?" Did she really have to ask?

"I said yes."

Bev leapt from the sofa and paced back and forth

like a caged tiger. "So . . . what you're telling me is . . . that you have . . . a date . . . with . . . a man."

"Bev, it's not really a date. It's Payne McAllister's Halloween party. Gary and I were both invited. He's going to pick me up and give me a ride there."

"He asked you two weeks in advance if you needed a ride to the party? Jesus, Andie, how deep in denial can you be? It's obviously a date!"

"Bev, it won't be a real date; it can't be. I mean, I'm not attracted to him or anything. I'm a dyke, for Chrissakes. It's just that —"

Bev wheeled around so that she was eyeball to eyeball with Andie. She knew her eyes were black with rage, but she didn't care. "It's just that what, Andie?"

"I . . . I," Andie stammered, trying to control her sobbing long enough to speak coherently. "I felt like I had to say yes because his dad's the dean and his mom's the director of admissions."

"I get it. So if you say no, he's going to run crying to his daddy and say, 'Daddy, Daddy, I think that Pritchard woman's a dyke because she won't go out with me.' So of course, his dad will say, 'Son, I guess we'll have to fire her then.' Is that what you think would happen, Andie?"

"I don't know. Maybe. You don't know how things are at little colleges like Randall. Everything's just so political."

"I might not know anything about colleges, but I do know one thing. If you were going to drag me all the way to southeastern Kentucky just to leave me for a man, I wish you'd told me ahead of time and saved me the time and the moving expenses!"

"Bev, you're being totally irrational. I'm not

leaving you for a man. I love you, Bev. I'm only going to this party with Gary because —"

"I know, I know. His dad's the dean. But what's next? 'I love you, Bev. I only kissed Gary because his dad's the dean.' 'I love you, Bev. I only fucked Gary because his dad's the dean.' 'I love you, Bev. I only married Gary because —' "

"Stop it, Bev!" Huge tears were rolling down Andie's cheeks. "You're scaring me."

"No." Bev was through yelling. Her voice was calm and even. "You're scaring me. When we moved in together seven years ago, I thought I was settling down with someone with personal integrity. I was obviously mistaken. Ever since we moved here, you've set up this big dividing line between your job and me. Your job's your public life, and I'm your dirty little secret —"

"Bev, no."

"You know it's true, Andie. And when you set up a dividing line like that, then eventually it has to come down to a choice: your job or me. And when Gary asked you out and you said yes, you made your choice."

"It's not like that —"

Bev couldn't listen anymore. She was tired of excuses, tired of charades. "Most of the stuff in the house is yours anyway. I'll take the futon, my clothes, my books. Kitty lang is yours; she was a present to you, but I might want to visit her sometimes . . . maybe when you're not home." Tears welled in Bev's eyes as she remembered Andie's birthday two years ago when they had gone to the animal shelter and adopted the tiny, mewing, three-color fuzzball who was soon dubbed kitty lang.

Adopting a pet together had been a symbol of their commitment. Bev wiped her eyes. No time for sentimentality; she had a lot of work to do. "If I start getting my stuff together now, I can be out of here for good by morning."

Andie was curled up in the fetal position on the sofa, weeping. "Bev, I swear I didn't know this was going to be that big a deal. Please . . . please don't leave me."

Bev couldn't let herself break, not now. "Andie, don't you understand? I didn't choose this. You did."

Chapter 13

Andie moved through her days with such cold precision that she began to wonder if *Andie* stood for Android instead of Andrea. Andie the Android — it was pretty funny actually. As kids in junior high used to say, so funny I forgot to laugh.

Mornings began at seven. She would get up, feed kitty lang, shower, dress, then force herself to consume a piece of dry toast and a cup of tea — sick person food. But that was okay, she was sick. Heartsick. Most of the time, she just felt numb. Classes in the morning, different sections of freshman composition, all the same. She explained the importance of thesis statements and well-organized essays as if she were doing it in her sleep. She held her office hours, graded her papers, and put on a cheerful mask when she saw her colleagues. They didn't know the difference; they just wanted to exchange pleasantries and move on. Pretty earrings. Nice weather. Working hard or hardly working?

When she went home in the evenings, she fed kitty lang again, heated up some prepackaged microwavable dinner, maybe read a little, went to bed early.

Weekends were harder. She told herself she would use the weekends to catch up on her sleep. But she was sleeping too much as it was.

The days passed slowly like the days of a jail sentence, and eventually it was the day of Payne Symington McAllister's Halloween party. She hadn't even thought about her costume. Virginia Woolf would be easy. She could put her hair up, wear her vintage dress and lace-up oxford shoes. She was lying on the sofa wondering if it would be too morbid to put rocks in her pockets when there was a knock at the door.

It was too early for Gary. As she got up, she hoped, just as she did every time the phone rang, that it was Bev. But when she opened the door, it was only Mamaw Needham.

"Hidy, honey," she said, waddling in without being asked. "I brung you a mess of greens. I seen you gettin' in your car the other day, and I thought you was lookin' kinda peaky. You been feelin' porely?"

"No, not really. I've been working awfully hard."

"Well, you eat you these greens." She handed Andie the pot. "And when you've eat the greens, drink off the juice that's left. That'll keep your strength up."

"Thank you." Andie could barely force herself to choke down her toast in the morning and frozen dinner in the evening, so the thought of drinking the juice from the pot of foul-smelling vegetable matter was nauseating.

It didn't take Mamaw Needham long to get to the real point of her visit. After she had settled down in her favorite chair, she asked, "Your cousin ain't livin' here no more, is she?"

"Um . . . no, she isn't."

"Y'all didn't have a fallin' out, did you?"

You can't cry, Andie told herself. Not in front of Mamaw Needham. "No, she just got that job, and she had enough money to get a place of her own."

"Well, I reckon that's all right. Now me, I ain't never lived all by myself in my life, and I don't think I could hardly stand it. I'm always happiest when there's a whole bunch around. Like when my boys was little, and the dogs and cats'd be in the house, and Ancil'd be home from work, and maybe he'd be playin' somethin' on the guitar, like 'Soldier's Joy' or the 'Wildwood Flower.' I've always loved 'Wildwood Flower.' The words don't make a lick of sense, but they sure sound purty. Anyway, I know some people'd say a noisy house like that'd get on their nerves, but I liked havin' all that life around. Course, you girls today is differ'nt — more independent-like."

Andie forced a weak smile. The truth was, she couldn't stand a quiet house either. "I guess so." She glanced down at her watch and felt a surge of panic.

"Mamaw, I hate to be rude, but I've got to get ready for a party."

"A party! Now that's somethin' I like. Who's a-havin' it?"

"Dr. McAllister from Randall."

Mamaw Needham flashed a mischievous, denture-filled grin. "I hope you ain't gonna be a wallflower at this party. You got a feller takin' you?"

"Yeah, a guy from the history department."

"Is he good lookin'?"

To be honest, Andie wasn't sure. "He's not bad."

"Looks ain't that important nohow. He treat you good?"

"Actually, I don't really know him that well. This is . . ." She stopped herself before she said "our first date." She refused to think of it as a date. "This is the first time we've really done anything together . . . besides just talk at work."

"A first date! Lord, I better get outta here and let you get yourself purtied up!" She squeezed Andie's hand on her way out. "I envy you, honey. It's such a blessin' to be young." As she negotiated the porch steps, she called, "You tell that cousin of yours to come by and see me. Just cause she ain't livin' here no more ain't no excuse for her to act like a stranger."

"I'll tell her," Andie said. If I ever talk to her again.

Andie the Android kicked in, mechanically going about the task of getting her costume ready for the party. Andie and Bev used to have Halloween parties in Boston — wild gatherings of dykes and gay boys and drag queens packed into their tiny apartment, laughing and guzzling rum punch that smoked evilly with dry ice. The two of them would always dress like famous couples; one year, Bev was Mark Antony and Andie was Cleopatra. Another year, they dressed as Boris and Natasha from *The Adventures of Rocky and Bullwinkle.*

I can't think about this, Andie told herself. It'll just make me more depressed, and I've got to get ready for this party. She put her hair up, zipped her dress, and tied her shoes. But in the end, it was not the hair or the dress that made her bear such a strong resemblance to Virginia Woolf; it was the deep sadness in her eyes.

Gary arrived dressed in full Civil War regalia — Confederate, of course.

"Let me guess," Andie said, smiling through clenched teeth. "Robert E. Lee."

"Close," Gary said, smiling for real. "Nathan Bedford Forrest."

What compatibility, Andie thought sarcastically. Virginia Woolf and Nathan Bedford Forrest — two hearts that could finally beat as one through the miracle of time travel. Wasn't it Nathan Bedford Forrest who founded the . . . ? Best not to think about it, she decided. "Well, Nathan, shall we go?"

"I guess we'd better. Virginia, right?"

"That's right."

"I knew it." Gary grinned, a little too pleased with himself.

When they walked out to his enormous gas-guzzler of a car, Andie was relieved to see an absence of Confederate-flag bumper stickers. Thank god for small favors, she thought. He opened the door on the passenger side with no small amount of ceremony. "Thanks," she mumbled. If someone had told her that by moving South, she would one day have the door of an aged Buick opened for her by a man in a Confederate uniform, she would have never believed it.

"Don't worry," Gary said. "You're out with a perfect gentleman."

Better not tell him that given the choice, she'd rather be out with a perfect lady.

Payne McAllister's home was a somewhat ostentatious fake colonial number on a street lined with other fake colonial numbers. The neighborhood looked like what would result if Thomas Jefferson had been brought back from the dead to design a subdivision on a limited budget.

Payne answered the door wearing a white shirt, snug black pants, and a brocade vest. His hair and mustache had been blackened with what appeared to be shoe polish. Andie couldn't figure out who he was supposed to be. Her best guess was Wayne Newton.

Payne extended his hand to Gary. "Pleased to make your acquaintance, sir," he boomed. "I'm Cap'n Rhett Butlah."

"Nathan Bedford Forrest, Cap'n."

Andie stood frozen in the doorway, watching the two Southern archetypes clasp hands.

Payne turned to Andie. "And you must be Virginia Woolf."

Andie was determined not to let the surrealism of this affair steal her identity. "Yes, Payne, I'm dressed as Virginia Woolf."

"Well, come in, y'all. Come in. Let me see if I

can find my Scahlett. Scahlett! Scahlett!" he called. Finally, a plump woman for whom fifty was a distant memory trotted over. She was wearing a brunette wig of ringlets and had managed to stuff her ample frame into a red antebellum gown like the one Vivien Leigh wore when Clark Gable carried her up the staircase. "This is my Scahlett, Louise McAllistah. Louise, you know Gary. This Virginia Woolf look-alike heah is Andrea Pritchard, ouah new faculty member."

"Lovely to meet you, Andrea," Louise said, curtsying grotesquely. She was obviously taking this whole Scarlett O'Hara thing far too seriously.

"These costumes wuh Louise's big idea," Payne said. "I think she was gettin' even with me foah my idea last yeah." He leaned toward Andie confidentially. "We went as the Snopeses."

"These costumes wuh just the hahdest thing in the wuhld to find," Louise said. "We had to ordah them all the way from Louville."

"They're stunning," Andie said. She certainly felt stunned.

Louise surveyed Andie and Gary's ensembles. "Payne and I thought that maybe y'all would weah matchin' costumes, too."

"Now, honey," Payne said. "This is just theah fuhst date." He chucked Gary on the shoulder playfully. "They can weah matchin' costumes next yeah."

Andie tried to smile, but all she could manage was to bare her teeth like an animal with its hackles up.

They mingled. Andie began chatting with Nina, who was dressed as Jane Austen. Gary offered to bring her a glass of neon-orange nonalcoholic punch, the only beverage that was being proffered at this gathering. When he disappeared to get it, Nina squeezed Andie's arm. "He's just a livin' doll, isn't he?"

Andie couldn't bring herself to call Gary, or anyone for that matter, a living doll. So instead she said, "He's a nice guy, all right."

Nina leaned over and stage-whispered, "I want you to look at what Inez has got on!" Nina pointed to the corner of the living room, where Inez, wearing a men's plaid suit and an odd houndstooth hat that perched on top of her head, was laughing with a man who appeared to be dressed as John Wayne.

"Who's she supposed to be?" Andie asked.

Nina rolled her eyes. "Coach Beah Bryant. I bet you don't know who he is, do you?"

"I don't really follow sports."

"Neithah do I, honey. Beah Bryant coached the UK and the Univuhsity of Alabama football teams. Inez loves college football bettuh than anything, and she just positively wuhshipped Beah Bryant. I tell you, Andrea, the day that man died, she cried like a baby. But anyway, we wuh tryin' to get our costumes togethuh, and she said she wanted to come as Beah Bryant. I said, 'Inez, honey, can't you think of anybody moah, you know, sophisticated?' And she said, 'It says right heah on the invitation to come as yoah favorite literary or historical figuh, and Beah Bryant is my favorite historical figuh. Besides, yoah costume is high-falutin' enough fuh the both of us!' I sweah, Andrea, sometimes I don't know what I'm gonna do with huh!" She looked over Andie's shoulder and smiled. "It looks like yoah gentleman friend has returned. I'll leave you two to talk."

Gary handed her one of the two cups of punch he was holding. He clinked his cup against hers in a sort of clumsy toast. "I got held up talking shop over by the punch bowl. I'm sorry I was gone so long."

"That's okay. I didn't mind." It was the first sincere thing she had said all evening.

Suddenly, Hill appeared before them. He was dressed in a Victorian-looking tweed suit. "Ah, Andrea," he said, nodding in Gary's direction. "Glad to see you're, ah, making friends." He looked around the room in apparent confusion. "You haven't seen my, ah, wife, Helen, have you? Short woman dressed like Elizabeth Barrett Browning?"

"I think she just went into the kitchen with Jane Austen," Andie said.

"Ah," Hill muttered and wandered away.

Bobby came up behind Andie and Gary and clapped them both on their backs. Andie jumped.

"Sorry, buddy, it's just me," Bobby said. "Gary, are you Nathan Bedford Forrest again this year?"

Gary smiled. "Are you Bobby Adkins again this year?"

Bobby looked down at the plain clothes he was wearing. "Yep. I never was the costume type. Always felt too damn silly. Even felt silly in my uniform in the army — it just wasn't me, you know? Hey, Andrea, have you met my wife?"

"I don't think I've had the pleasure."

Bobby gestured to the woman who had been standing slightly behind him. She had straight brown hair so long she could probably sit on it. She was wearing plain clothes, too, jeans and a sweater. "Andrea, this is Sharon. Sharon's not the costume type either, are you, honey?"

She smiled shyly. "Not really. It's nice to meet you, Andrea. Bobby talks a lot about you. He says you're real funny once you get loosened up."

Andie laughed. "Well, nobody has to loosen Bobby up, do they, Sharon?"

"Shoot, no," Sharon laughed. "Now getting him to shut up, that's another matter."

Bobby draped his arm around his wife amiably. "She's mean to me, Andrea, but I love her." He looked at Sharon fondly. "You ready to go, hon? We just stopped by to say hey."

Andie could hardly bear to be around a couple as well-matched as Bobby and Sharon. She and Bev had been that good a match once.

About half an hour after all the guests had arrived, the party became sexually segregated. No one stood up and announced that all the men would stay in the living room and talk, while all the women would settle in the den, and yet that is exactly what happened. There was only one exception to the unofficial rule — Inez Ratliff, who stayed in the living room and talked with the men.

Andie had mixed feelings about this turn of events. She was relieved because it separated her from Gary. At the same time, the arrangement put her in a room full of strangers, with the exception of Nina. And the conversation in that circle was of such a domestic bent that she couldn't help but wonder if the men and Inez were having a better time.

"Have any of you had a chance to shop at the new Value-Mart?" Helen Hill asked.

"I went the othah day," Mrs. Symington said. "It's a gohgeous stoah, but I thought theah produce was too high."

“It seems like produce is highuh than a cat’s back wherevuh you go,” Nina said. “Of coahse, I’ve not been to the Value-Maht. I’ve been shoppin’ at the IGA for twenty yeahs, and I guess I’m just set in my ways.” She turned to Andie in an obvious attempt to bring her into the conversation. “Wheah do you do yoah shoppin’, Andrea?”

“I like the Value-Mart better than the IGA,” she answered halfheartedly. “Selection is better, I think.”

The conversation on grocery shopping continued for nearly forty more minutes. Andie couldn’t believe it. The most fascinating conversations she had ever participated in had taken place among groups of women, and yet here were these women, dressed to represent two of the greatest writers of the nineteenth century, Jane Austen and Elizabeth Barrett Browning, and one of the strongest women in literature, Scarlett O’Hara, and all they could find to talk about was the price of produce. Andie had to wonder if such banalities were really all they could think of to discuss or if they purposely stuck to what they thought were appropriate and safe topics.

Andie looked over at Nina. If she was as bored as Andie by the idle chatter, she didn’t show it.

Andie listened to the women hold forth on the subjects of children and church — two topics she was particularly useless on since she liked children but had none and disliked churches so attended none. When Gary appeared in the doorway and asked if she was ready to go, she was actually relieved, simply because he represented an opportunity for escape.

In the car on the way to Andie’s house, Gary said, “I’m sorry we didn’t get a chance to talk more.”

“That’s okay. Do parties here always split up like

that, with the women in one room and the men in the other?"

"They usually do. It works out that way naturally, I think. Since men and women are different, they like to talk about different things."

Andie never understood this argument from heterosexuals. If men and women were so different that they had nothing to say to each other, then why did they pair off together in the first place? She decided not to pursue this line of thought. "What did you menfolk talk about?"

"Work mostly, some sports."

Color me surprised, thought Andie.

"What did you womenfolk talk about?"

"Cute boys, feminine hygiene, that kind of thing."

Gary looked shocked, then gave in and laughed. "You're kind of . . . irreverent, aren't you?"

Andie smiled patiently. What a goofball. "Irreverent, irrelevant, you name it."

They pulled into the driveway of Andie's house. "Say," Gary said. "I don't know if you'd be interested, but I'm singing in church on Sunday. Would you like to come?"

An invitation to church. It had to happen sooner or later. "I didn't know you sang."

"Just a little. I'm in the choir, but I'm doing a solo. What do you say?"

I'd rather have all my teeth pulled without anesthesia, Andie thought. "Sure, I'd love to hear you sing."

"Great. I'll pick you up Sunday at nine-forty-five in the morning."

"I figured it was in the morning."

"Would you like me to walk you to your door?"

"No, that's okay. Thanks, though." Andie could tell that Gary was debating some display of affection. She opened the car door in hopes of curtailing it. "Good night, Gary."

"Good night, Andrea."

When she walked into the dark house, there was only kitty lang to greet her.

Chapter 14

Had it not been for Wanda, Bev would have spent her first night away from Andie on one of the bedraggled sofas in the Kaffeeklatsch Korner. Staying with Cricket wasn't an option, since his apartment, however luxurious, was only large enough to accommodate the most intimate of overnight guests. Staying at one of Morgan's two motels was a possibility, but she didn't really want to shell out the money since she was going to have to come up with a security deposit on a new place to live. It was hard to know what to do. She just sat behind the cash register in the thrift store, dazed by the fact that she had walked out on a seven-year relationship.

The bell on the front door jingled. It was 11:00 o'clock — time for Wanda to come in for her cup of coffee and three cigarettes. She didn't even bother with a greeting. "Bev, what you got your truck all loaded up for?"

Bev's truck, filled with all her worldly possessions, was parked outside the Mountain Women's Outreach Center. In the rare moments when she wasn't brooding about Andie, she said a silent prayer against theft and rain. "I just moved out of where I was living."

"Where you movin' to?"

"I don't know."

Wanda settled down in the Kaffeeklatsch Korner and lit her first cigarette. "Seems to me that movin' out that quick without even knowin' where you're movin' to can only mean one thing."

Bev was distracted but trying to pay attention. "What's that?"

Wanda exhaled a long stream of smoke. "Man trouble."

Bev wondered if she should let Wanda's assumption go unchallenged. No, that's what Andie would do. She walked over to the sofa and sat down across from the woman she hoped was her friend. "Actually, Wanda, there is something else it can mean."

"What's that?"

"Woman trouble."

"Now, honey, I don't see what your female parts has got to do with this, unless . . . Honey, did you find out you're barren?"

"Not that kind of woman trouble. I meant I was having trouble with another woman. Wanda, I think of you as my friend, and I hope you won't want to stop being my friend because of this, but I'm the kind of woman who doesn't like to, you know, date men. I like other women."

Wanda's eyes widened in surprise and comprehension. "Oh." She took a long draw on her cigarette. "I heard tell of women like that."

"I've been with this same woman for seven years. We lived together like we were married, and I moved here with her from Boston. I love her — loved her — the same way I imagine you love Joe." She bit her lip hard, trying not to cry. "The thing is, Wanda, yesterday — last night, really — we broke up."

"Hmm." Wanda stubbed out her cigarette and lit another one. "I reckon you must be feelin' pretty bad right now."

Bev heaved an involuntary sigh of relief. "Yeah."

"Where you sleepin' at tonight?"

"I don't know. Here, I guess."

"You don't need to be stayin' here all by yourself of a night. We got a couch that folds out into a bed at the house. You could stay there tonight."

"Oh, Wanda, I couldn't —"

"Look, Bev. You been real good to Tammy and me, and it ain't none of my business who you run around with, long as you ain't after neither one of us. And I figure you ain't cause what would you want with a dried-up old granny and a pregnant girl?"

Bev cracked a smile.

"So you come on over to the house after you get offa work. Hit's one-twelve Cotton Street. I'll tell

Tammy everything when she comes home from school. But if it's all right, honey, I might just tell Joe that you left your husband. He'd understand about a woman leavin' her husband better'n he would about a woman —"

"Leaving her wife?"

Wanda looked a little embarrassed. "Yeah. So you jus' come on after work then."

"Wanda, are you sure this is —"

"Now, Bev, I done told you to come on. I ain't takin' no for an answer."

Wanda's house was tiny, just four small rooms. The furniture was threadbare, but everything was meticulously clean. Joe was sleeping in a battered recliner in the corner of the living room. His face was sharp and angular, and his breath came in great gasps despite the tubing from the oxygen machine that fed into his nose. "He sleeps a whole lot," Wanda whispered to Bev. She gestured to the oxygen machine, which looked incongruously high-tech in the modestly furnished living room. "If you wanna smoke, you'll have to do it outside 'cause of that thing. Light a cigarette in here, and the whole house'd blow up."

"I don't mind going outside. It keeps me from smoking too much."

Wanda walked into the kitchen, and Bev followed her. "I'm fixin' us some supper," she said, stirring a pot of what appeared to be beans. "Tammy's in the back if you wanna go say hey to her."

Tammy was lying across her bed on her stomach

reading an American history textbook. She rested her chin on the body of a raggedy teddy bear.

"I didn't mean to interrupt your studying," Bev said.

"That's okay. The test ain't 'til Thursday. I was just tryin' to study ahead a little." She lifted herself up into a sitting position. "Whew, I ain't gonna be able to lay on my belly like that much longer." She patted a spot on the bed next to her, the only other sitting place in the room. "Nanny told me what happened."

"Yeah."

"You look like you been cryin'."

Bev had hoped it wasn't obvious. "I turned on the waterworks on my way over here. I was good at work. I didn't cry all day, so of course, I burst into tears the second I got into my truck."

"Nanny said y'all'd been together a real long time."

"Seven years."

"Shoot, that is a long time. What happened?"

"I don't know. Moving here was part of it. It's hard having a relationship that most people don't approve of."

"I guess so. I never met nobody like you before, a girl who likes girls, I mean."

"I'm just glad that you and your grandma aren't judgmental about it."

Tammy laughed and patted her tummy. "Honey, as many people as I've got in this town judgin' me, I don't reckon I orta be judgin' nobody myself.

Bev smiled. "Tammy, what happened to the father of your baby?"

She shrugged. "Same thing that happens to the father of a lot of girls's babies. He told me he loved me before we done it, then he said it wasn't his and took off."

"Did you love him?"

"Wouldn'ta done it if I hadn't loved him."

They sat in silence for a moment, Bev contemplating her solitude, Tammy seeming to do much the same thing. But Tammy wasn't really alone, Bev thought. She had her grandmother and the life growing in her belly. Bev had nothing but a truckload of worthless possessions.

"Hey, I know what!" Tammy said, brightening suddenly. "I got a paper. Why don't we go through the classifieds and see if we can find you a place to live?"

Bev did find a place that kept her from having to rely on the kindness of Wanda and Tammy for another night. It was a tiny efficiency apartment — one cheaply paneled room with a kitchenette and a tiny bathroom with a cracked, mildewed shower stall. One window provided a panoramic view of a brick wall. Bev took the apartment partially because of the view, which she considered symbolic.

Cricket was appalled the first time he saw the apartment and returned on his second visit with red curtains, colorful throw pillows for the futon, and a huge Frida Kahlo print. "Just 'cause you're wallowin' in misery is no reason to be tacky," he said. Bev let him arrange things as he wished; though to be honest, she didn't want the apartment to seem homey. She only wanted it to be a place where she could collapse in exhaustion after a long day's work.

Bev threw herself into her work at the center. She instituted the "bag sale" at the thrift store; customers could purchase all the clothing they could cram in a paper grocery bag for one dollar. She advertised the sale on the radio and in the newspaper, and for the first time women poured in. She insisted that all the women who came to the bag sale fill out a survey saying what services they would like the center to provide. When many of the women claimed to have left their glasses at home, Bev talked to Teresa about the possibility of the center offering adult literacy tutoring.

The more time and energy she put into work, the less she had to think about how much she missed Andie and how she would almost be willing to go back to being her dirty little secret just to be with her again. She taught her nutrition and childcare class with unbridled enthusiasm; only Wanda and Tammy could sense that her perky exterior was a mask for her misery. The class was going extremely well; only one thing concerned Bev — the absence of Jeanie, whom she hadn't seen since the night she had unsuccessfully offered to help her.

That state of affairs soon changed, however. One Friday evening, Bev was walking up the stairs to her apartment with a case of beer she had traveled across the state line to purchase when she saw a red-haired girl walking down the hall. Bev picked up her pace. "Jeanie?" she called.

The girl turned around. "Oh, it's you," she said, sounding far from thrilled. "What're you doin' here?"

"I haven't been trailing you, if that's what you think," Bev said. "I live here now. Apartment three."

"How come a do-gooder like you is livin' in a dump like this?"

"If I recall correctly, the last time I inquired into your life, you pretty much let it be known that it was none of my damn business. So maybe this is —"

Jeanie looked as if she might smile, but didn't. "None of my damn business?"

"That's right. I do know something that's both of our business, though, and that's why you haven't been coming to class."

"Say, is them beers you got? Can I have one of 'em?"

"If you had been coming to class, you'd know that it is bad for you to drink while you're pregnant — both for you and the baby."

"Well, thanks for the health bulletin. I gotta go."

"Wait." Bev didn't want to lose her. "Maybe if you come to my apartment, I could set you up with a glass of orange juice or something."

Jeanie's smirk implied that she didn't find this offer particularly attractive. "That's okay. Like I said, I gotta go."

"Look, Jeanie. I know I pissed you off the last time we talked. And I think I know why, too. You think that because I offered to help you I think I'm better than you. Well that's bullshit. I'm as fucked up as the next person, or maybe more so right now."

She ran her fingers through her hair in exasperation. "I thought you needed somebody to talk to. If you don't, I apologize heartily for my mistake, and I'll just go on to my apartment and drink my beer in peace."

Bev thought she heard Jeanie whisper something.

"What?"

"I said I'm sorry. I'm sorry I was ugly to you, okay? I've just not been real happy lately."

"That's okay. I know the feeling. Why don't you come in and have that juice now?"

Jeanie rolled her eyes at the idea, but said, "Okay."

Bev was relieved to see that there was still some orange juice in the fridge. She didn't keep track of her groceries much these days since she didn't have much of an appetite. Cooking for one didn't seem worth the trouble. When her stomach growled so loudly it got on her nerves, she'd eat a cup of yogurt or some peanut butter and crackers and leave it at that.

Jeanie was staring at the print on the wall when Bev brought her juice. "She's just got one eyebrow," Jeanie said. "Looks like you'd wanna shave a little space in the middle or somethin'."

"That's Frida Kahlo," Bev said. "She painted a lot of self-portraits. My friend Cricket gave me that picture. He said he had it up in his bedroom, but he felt like she was staring at him all the time."

"Cricket Needham?"

"Yeah."

"He's a queer, you know."

"So?" Bev said a little too defensively.

"So nothin'. I just thought you orta know." She

flopped down on the futon. Bev sat across from her on the floor, not wanting to get too close after that last comment.

"Did you stop coming to class because you were pissed off at me?"

"That was pretty much it."

"Pretty much?"

Jeanie set down her glass. "I swear to God, I believe you are the nosiest person I ever seen in my life."

"I probably am. Look, Jeanie, I worry about you. The other women in the class have the support of their families. You're the youngest mother in class, and I've never heard you say a word about your family. You work full-time and you live in this crappy building. It's not just that I want to know what your story is because I'm nosy. I need to know, for your own good, if you're ready to have this baby and take care of it. Jeanie, you'll have to take care of this kid for eighteen years. Jesus, you've not even lived eighteen years!" Bev leaned over to look her directly in the eyes. "Look, if you can honestly tell me that you're ready — emotionally, mentally, financially — to have this baby, I promise I'll leave you alone."

When Jeanie looked up, there were tears in her eyes. "I don't know. I don't know if I even want to."

"Jeanie, you don't live here with your family, do you?"

"My daddy kicked me out of the house when I told him I was pregnant. I told him . . . I told him it wasn't my fault. I told him I didn't even wanna do what got me pregnant in the first place."

"Do you mean you were raped?"

"I don't know if that's what you'd call it or not. My cousin . . . he's older, and he's always . . . doin' things to me. He always tells me not to say nothin' about it, and I never did . . . 'til this happened."

"Where's your cousin now?"

"He took off after he found out I was pregnant. I don't know where he is. Don't care neither."

"Jeanie, you don't have to have this baby."

She snorted. "God, I might as well shoot myself in the head as get rid of it. My daddy'll throw me out of the house for gettin' knocked up, but he'd kill me for . . . for . . . well, you know."

"That's awfully unfair, isn't it? He won't help you when you're pregnant, but he'll kill you if you get an abortion. Jeanie, I don't want to pressure you into a decision, but if you don't want a baby yet — particularly given the circumstances under which you got pregnant, you don't need to have it."

"I don't want it, okay? But I also don't wanna get killed, and I also don't have no money."

"Don't worry about the money. And if anybody asks you what happened, just say you didn't carry to term. It'll be the truth; it just simply makes it sound like a miscarriage. I don't want to pressure you into a decision. Think about this. Decide what you want to do."

"I know what I wanna do. Are you really gonna help me?"

"If you recall, that's what I told you I wanted to do in the first place."

"I know, I know."

"I'm going to help you take care of this under two conditions. One, I better see you in the GED preparation class in the spring. Two, when you decide to become a mother, if you decide to become a mother, be a good one. Deal?"

"Deal."

"Okay, then, I'll see what I can do."

"Bev?"

"Yeah?"

"Can I have one of them beers now?"

Chapter 15

Gary cut his steak in umpteen million little pieces and doused it in ketchup before he started eating it. Andie mentally added this little habit to her ever-growing list of things about Gary that drove her absolutely insane. This one fell under the annoying-personal-quirks section, a section which also included such complaints as tooth-sucking and nails-never-quite-clean.

They were eating at the steakhouse where she and Bev had their last meal out together. Andie had nearly bitten through her lip when the hostess seated them at the table under the deer's head. She had halfheartedly made her crack about eating with Bambi staring at them, which had only succeeded in getting Gary off on a tangent about his love of deer hunting, a subject he seemed intent on staying on for the duration of their meal.

"And of course, there was the time when some ol' boys I know went deer hunting, and they sat under a tree and waited and waited. And finally, they waited so long they fell asleep. And when they woke up . . ." He paused to snort with laughter; snorts-when-laughs was also on Andie's annoying quirks list. "When they woke up, there wasn't a deer to be seen, but there were deer droppings right at their feet!" He slapped the table, overcome by mirth.

Andie was losing her patience. "You know, I just don't get deer hunting. I mean, what's so manly and sportsmanlike about shooting a beautiful, gentle animal whose only line of defense is to stare at you with big, brown eyes?"

Gary smiled at her adoringly. "I'm sorry, Andie. I'd forgotten how softhearted city women can be about animals."

His response was typical. In the past couple of weeks, their interaction had taken on a distinct pattern: he would say something that pissed her off, she would verbally eviscerate him, and he would adore her all the more for it. Andie's hope was always that if she disagreed with him loudly and often enough, he would decide that she was too opinionated and wouldn't want to see her anymore. Unfortunately, this was never the effect her verbal combativeness had. Instead, it endeared her to him, made him think of her as "feisty."

After dinner they went to a movie, one of those glossy Hollywood heteromances designed for straight couples out on dates. Andie didn't follow the plot of the movie; it wasn't interesting enough to hold her attention. The leading lady was too skinny and had an enormous amount of hair and a mouthful of huge, perfectly white teeth. The leading man kept his eyes squinted up in a bad imitation of James Dean. That was all she really noticed about the film; she spent most of her time in the darkened theater brooding about what a hopeless mess her life was.

It was the fifth time she and Gary had gone out together. She still refused to call the outings *dates,* even though it was increasingly apparent that that was what they were.

Going to church with him had been the worst. The first time, when she had gone to hear him sing a solo, had been positively terrifying. She had walked into the sanctuary of that huge Baptist church downtown to see Dr. and Mrs. Hill and Nina and Inez and Payne McAllister and his wife and Joyce and her mother and Gary's mom and dad all sitting in the pews, smiling at her. She had felt like an innocent newcomer to a small town in one of those horror novels in which the town is populated by members of some bizarre religious cult. If they had put her in a white robe and sacrificed her, she wouldn't have been at all surprised.

But what actually happened might have been worse. She had to listen to Gary belt out "How Great Thou Art" in his off-key baritone voice and suffer through a sermon on instilling moral values in one's children. Afterward, everyone from Randall had come up and shaken her hand or patted her shoulder, saying "We're so glad you could come" and "Wasn't it a lovely service?" and "Doesn't Gary have a beautiful voice?" The subtext had been clear: "You're playing the game well, my dear. Keep playing your cards right, and you can be one of us." One of us. Fitting in was easy, as long as you were willing to sacrifice your identity to do it.

The woman on the screen with all the hair and teeth was crying. Andie felt as though she might cry, too. She hadn't spoken to Bev since the night they broke up. She had called the Mountain Women's Outreach Center once to hear her voice, but Teresa had answered and Andie had hung up. She decided not to let herself cry. It was best for now not to think about Bev, best not to stir things up internally or externally. In her doctoral program, she had learned one lesson: Careers are hard to come by; do what you can to insure yours. And what would insure a career in Morgan was social approval. She could not get over the amount of social approval her feigned relationship with Gary had generated. Last week they had dinner with Gary's parents. Next week, they were invited to a pre-Thanksgiving dinner at Mamaw Needham's house, so Mamaw could "get a good look at this feller."

The thing that worried her was, could she win this game and insure her career and then go back to being herself and maybe even go back to Bev, if Bev would have her? Or was this a game that never really ended, that just had to be played and replayed until retirement or death, whichever came first? A hand reached over and clasped hers. It was big and rough with stiff hairs growing on its back, not soft and small like Bev's had been. Her first instinct was to pull away from the offensive paw, but then she realized it belonged to Gary. Bev's mocking words echoed in her head. "I love you, Bev. I only kissed Gary because his dad's the dean." But another voice overrode Bev's: Preserve your career, it said. Andie held Gary's hand. She disliked the feel of the hand as much as she disliked the person to whom it was attached. But that was okay. She didn't like herself much either.

Chapter 16

Cricket had arranged to take care of Jeanie's problem with one phone call. When Bev explained to him that Jeanie didn't need to deal with the trauma or expense of driving all the way to Lexington to a women's clinic, he had stared at his nails thoughtfully for a minute, then said he thought he knew someone local who could do it. When Bev asked about the money, he had said, "Don't worry about the money, sweetie. The ol' boy I'm fixin' to call owes the Needhams a favor."

When he got off the phone, he had said, "Okay.

Dr. Mayfield says he'll do it. But here's the thing you have to tell Jeanie. He said, 'Under no circumstances will this procedure be called an *abortion.* I don't perform abortions. This is an emergency D and C.' "

"But a dilation and curettage usually is an abortion."

"Honey, I know that, and you know that, but most of the people in Morgan don't. Besides an emergency D and C sounds much more . . . necessary, don't you think?"

So Bev had taken Jeanie to Dr. Mayfield's office and had sat in the waiting room while the procedure was being performed, dying for a cigarette and wishing there was something to read besides outdated issues of *Good Housekeeping* and *Field and Stream.* When the nurse came into the waiting room and motioned to her, Bev followed her down the hallway and found Jeanie resting in a hospital bed in the last room on the left. Bev had wondered how many women had recuperated in that bed after so-called "emergency D and C's."

When Bev took Jeanie back home and tucked her into her own bed, she asked, "Jeanie, do you remember my mentioning my friend Cricket Needham?"

"The queer? Yeah. I remember."

"It was Cricket who arranged for you to see Dr. Mayfield."

"What for? He don't even know me."

"I told him about you, and he wanted to help you. Jeanie, I want you to remember that when you were in trouble and had nobody to turn to, two queers helped you out."

That had been yesterday. Now it was Friday evening, and Bev had done her good deeds for the week. She lay on the futon in her apartment, drinking a can of beer and listening to Joni Mitchell on the scratchy old record player she had picked up at the thrift store. She hated drinking alone. She hated doing anything alone, really, but she didn't have the energy to go out and find company. Besides, she didn't want just anybody's company. The other day at work, she had called Andie's when she knew she wouldn't be home just so she could listen to her voice on the answering machine. Pathetic. She was pathetic. Sure, she might fill her weekdays with meaningful work, but evenings and weekends she took a nosedive into the proverbial well of loneliness. She got up to turn the record over and was startled by a knock at the door.

It was Cricket, dressed to the teeth in a loose purple silk shirt and black pants that were tucked into knee-high purple suede boots. He swept into the room. "Put on your dancin' shoes, honey! We're goin' *out!* "

Bev looked down at her current ensemble, a faded black pocket T-shirt and gray sweatpants. "Out?"

"Yes, out. I bet you've not been out in so long you don't even know what *out* means. Lord, girl, all you do when you're not at work is lie around this trashy apartment and mope, mope, mope. Well, I'm sick of it. Where's your closet, woman? We've got to get some real clothes on you!" Cricket, who knew damned well where her closet was, went straight to it and started pulling out outfits, shaking his head, and hanging them back up. "Wait," he said finally, pulling out a white western-style shirt and black jeans. "This, I think."

"And where, pray tell, are we going?" Bev asked, taking the clothing obediently and stepping out of her sweatpants. She could change in front of Cricket. It wasn't like her body held any particular interest for him.

"There's a gay bar down in Odessa. I thought you might like to check it out."

"Cricket, are you trying to lure me out so I can meet new women? Because if you are, I'm not interested."

Cricket fluttered his eyelashes with exaggerated innocence. "Why, of course I'm not tryin' to get you to meet somebody else. Everybody knows you're my girlfriend. Speakin' of that, Mamaw Needham wants you and me to come over Wednesday for some kind of pre-Thanksgiving supper. Are you up for it?"

"You're quite the busy little social secretary, aren't you? Do we have to hold hands and act all kissypoo?"

"We don't have to act no way. Mamaw'll draw her own conclusions. She always does."

Bev had put on the shirt and pants, along with a black leather belt and her black "cowdyke" boots. "Do I look okay?"

"Just run a brush through your hair, and you'll be fabulous. Come on, honey. I am dyin' to get out of this town!"

Bev brushed her hair as instructed and took two beers out of the fridge. Soon they were speeding down the interstate, growing more and more intoxicated with freedom the farther away they got from Morgan.

"Where is Odessa anyway?"

"It's in Tennessee. You cross the state line, then go across three counties."

"Jesus. You know, I actually used to live right across the street from a gay bar."

Odessa, Tennessee, did not have any of the makings of a gay mecca. The downtown was as small as Morgan's and perhaps even a little more rundown. Bev thought Cricket should be parking soon. In her experience, most gay bars were located downtown. But he just kept on driving. Soon they were on a country road so winding that the beer in Bev's stomach sloshed around ominously. "Cricket, there isn't a gay bar out here. This is like one of those tricks you rural types play on city folk, right? You're not going to take me snipe hunting, are you? Because I know that trick."

Cricket laughed. "Just you wait." He turned down a wooded side road. They passed a tiny, white church and the first real tarpaper shack Bev had ever seen. A gay bar on Tobacco Road. Who'd have thought it? Cricket turned down another road, this one gravel and leading into a grove of trees.

"Is this the part where the crazed Vietnam vet jumps out and kills us?"

"You city people are so paranoid. We're just about there."

Past the grove of trees, in the clearing, was a small, concrete-block building with a hand-painted sign that read *The Hideaway*. You couldn't say it wasn't aptly named.

Were it not for its patrons, the interior of The Hideaway could easily be mistaken for a small-town redneck bar. The walls were cheaply paneled and decorated with neon beer signs. There were a pool table and a jukebox and a disconcertingly sticky floor. The bartender, a well-groomed, middle-aged man wearing an expensive-looking magenta sport shirt, was the first clue that this was no ordinary rural watering hole.

Bev stood there as if her boots were glued to the floor (which, as a matter of fact, they were), trying to reassure herself that this was indeed a gay bar and therefore a place where she belonged. It was so different from the teal-and-pink art deco hangouts she was used to that she found herself coming down with a bad case of culture shock.

Cricket took her by the arm. "Let's go over to the bar. I'll introduce you to Doug."

Doug, as it turned out, was the well-groomed barkeep. He reached out to half-hug Cricket. "You're looking stunning as always, Cricket. Who's your friend?"

"This is Bev. She just moved to Morgan from Boston."

Doug clucked his tongue sympathetically. "I'm sure that's been a learning experience. So, Bev, how does our little place compare to your bars in Bean Town?"

Bev searched for something nice to say. "It's . . . it's . . . incomparable."

Doug laughed. "Very diplomatic! You realize, of course, that this isn't how I'd decorate the place if I could do it up any way I wanted. But around these parts, it doesn't pay to be too swishy. Especially when Odessa's finest decide to pay us a visit. The concrete block, the paneling, the beer signs . . . just think of it all as protective coloration."

Bev laughed. "Is running the bar what you do for a living?" She couldn't imagine there was much money in it. The place wasn't exactly packed.

"Lord, no. I only open it up on weekends. Let's just say I think of The Hideaway as my community service project. I lose a bundle on it, but a lot of people around here would go nuts without it, myself included. By day, I'm a mild-mannered dentist, pillar of the Odessa community, sort of like Cricket is in Morgan — the respectable town fairy."

Cricket giggled. "Not half as many people in Odessa know about you. Everybody in Morgan knows about me."

Doug winked at him. "No offense, dear, but how could they not?" He turned to Bev. "The tradition here is that new visitors get their first drink on the house. What'll it be?"

"Beer's fine, thanks."

"All right, then, one beer for Bev, and I already know that the princess here wants a fuzzy navel."

As they walked away from the bar, Cricket said, "Doug's a great guy. We went out a couple of times."

"Why not more?"

"We liked each other and everything. We just didn't hit it off, you know, that way."

Only two other women were in the Hideaway, and from the looks of it, they were unaware that anybody else was in the bar but them. They were pressed close against each other, slow dancing to a mournful country song on the jukebox. They were as butch-femme as pseudodykes Inez and Nina, though they were nearly thirty years younger. The butch's hair was long in back but buzz-cut on the top and sides. She was stocky and wore a button-down shirt with a tie. Her hands were adorned with homemade tattoos. You don't mess with a woman with tattoos on her hands, Bev thought. The butch's girlfriend had enormously permed hair and was wearing jeans, but with a pink sweater and pearls and high heels.

The men in the bar were mostly effeminate and exquisitely dressed. The Hideaway was apparently the gathering place for all the Crickets from all the small towns in southeastern Kentucky and northeastern Tennessee.

One particularly energetic young man bounded up and embraced Cricket, squealing, "Hey, girl! How you doin'?"

"I'm pretty good, Ken. How 'bout you?" Cricket responded with uncharacteristic coolness.

"Girl, I have never been better." Ken clapped his hands joyously. "I'm fixin' to get out of this little hellhole of a town. I got me a job down in Knoxville at this place where they take hotel reservations? That town is full of faggots, honey. They've got three gay bars there. Three of 'em. And you know what the main drag downtown is called?"

"Gay Street," Cricket said, dripping boredom.

"That's right, honey! I'm fixin' to be a city girl now!"

After Ken walked away, Cricket muttered, "That town'll eat that faggot alive." A heavy, middle-aged man in a fedora waved to Cricket from a booth in the back corner. "There's Stanley. Let's go sit with him. You'll love him."

"Cricket!" Stanley boomed. "How goes it, dear boy? Embalmed any interesting corpses lately?"

"Nope, most of 'em are pretty quiet. Course, that's more'n I can say about you."

Stanley chortled. "Touché, my boy." He nodded toward Bev. "And who is this striking amazon?"

"I'm Bev."

"Well, Bev, Cricket, sit down, sit down. We might as well settle in for a long winter's chat because there's certainly nothing doing tonight."

"Stanley's the city librarian over in Jericho," Cricket explained to Bev.

A librarian. Well, that explained the high-blown speech. "What's it like being a librarian in a small town —"

"Where people would rather burn books than read them? It's a constant challenge, I'll tell you that." He peered over Bev's shoulder. "Well, well, well. Something just walked in that should strike your fancy, Cricket."

"Really? Where?"

"He's over at the bar now. Be subtle."

Cricket whipped his head around toward the bar, then looked back at Bev and Stanley and emitted a piercing squeal of delight.

"Nice subtlety," Bev said.

"Our young Cricket is the queen of subtlety, don't you think, Bev?"

Cricket stamped his purple-booted feet under the table excitedly. "Look at him, Bev! Just look at him!"

Bev was curious to see what Cricket's type might

be. When she glanced at the bar, she saw a man who seemed to be as big as a mountain. With his black beard and checked shirt and boots, he resembled no one so much as Paul Bunyan. "Jesus," Bev said. "Do you think he parked his blue ox outside?"

Stanley let out another chortle, then said to Cricket, "An amusing amazon you've found here."

Cricket ignored him. "He couldn't possibly be gay, could he? Men who look like that never are — at least not around here."

Seconds later, Doug arrived at their table and set another fuzzy navel in front of Cricket. "From the gentleman at the bar," he said.

Cricket's face turned the same shade of magenta as Doug's shirt. "Omigod!" he screamed.

"Don't just sit there giggling like a schoolgirl," Stanley said. "Invite the nice man over to our table."

"I just couldn't. He'll probably hate me. I just wouldn't know what to say to a man like that —"

While Cricket continued his fit of insecurity, Bev got up from the booth, walked over to the giant at the bar, and said, "My friend over there would like to invite you to join us."

The giant grinned. "Your cute little blonde friend?"

"That's the one."

He chucked Bev on the shoulder. "Thanks, Hoss."

He squeezed himself into the booth beside Cricket, and Bev slid in beside Stanley. "Hey," the giant said. "I'm Wayne."

Bev liked Wayne instantly. He was huge but gentle-natured, like a Rottweiler who looks vicious but is really just an affectionate puppy at heart. Wayne said he drove a coal truck for a living and admitted that he had only recently gotten up enough nerve to come to The Hideaway. "But," he added, nodding in Cricket's direction, "I'm sure glad I did." Wayne was at his most doglike when looking at Cricket, his liquid brown eyes filled with utter devotion, a Rottweiler entranced by a tiny toy poodle. Soon the two of them were up and dancing to "It Wasn't God Who Made Honky-Tonk Angels."

"Oh, I hope this turns out to be something wonderful for Cricket," Stanley gushed. "He's such a sweet boy, but he hasn't been very lucky in love."

Bev took a gulp of beer. "Who has been?"

"I didn't realize that the Amazon Cricket brought with him was also a Cynic. What are you doing, dear — going about town with a lantern searching for an honest woman?"

"Well, I moved down here with a woman, only she turned out not to be too honest."

"I see. Well, why don't I buy us another round, and you can tell Uncle Stanley all about it."

Bev did tell Stanley all about it. She talked through three more rounds of drinks, talked until Doug pulled the cord on the jukebox and announced that it was time for the live entertainment. "What? They've got a drag show here or something?" Bev slurred. She was as drunk as she had been in a long time.

"That's a bit too sophisticated for here. It's probably just that awful country singer woman again. That's the one thing I detest about coming here. I simply cannot abide country music — all that twanging and whining about cheating hearts and so forth."

It was a country singer. Doug said that her name

was Rhonda Dudney. She was a bleached blonde in her forties and not conventionally beautiful at all. With her sharp jaw and her finely lined face, she was what some people might call hard looking. Her voice fit her appearance perfectly. Her accompanist hit the first plinking notes of "Faded Love" on the old upright piano in the corner, and she half-croaked, half-sang the lyrics.

"She bellows like an old mule," Stanley said.

That was true on one level, and yet Rhonda's singing was like a jagged blade that cut right into Bev's heart. She sang not with the voice of an experienced singer, but with the voice of experience — with the voice of someone who had loved and lost.

"She understands," Bev said. "She knows what it's like."

"Don't get all mushy on me," Stanley said. "That's just the beer talking, and you know it. That's what country music is designed to do, you know, make people who have drunk too much feel sorry for themselves."

Despite Stanley's cautionary statements, she sent Rhonda a drink. She ached to talk with a woman who could understand even a little bit of what she was feeling. After Rhonda's set was over, she came over to their table.

"Goodness me. Look at how late it's gotten," Stanley said as soon as Rhonda arrived. "I must be off to fight the battle of Jericho. I suppose I'll just go over and interrupt Cricket and Wayne's billing and cooing long enough to say good night. Bev, it was lovely meeting you. Do give me a call sometime. I'd love to make you dinner. Good night." He leaned over and whispered in Bev's ear, "And be careful."

"That man's in here ever' weekend and he never says so much as boo to me," Rhonda said after Stanley left.

"He's a nice guy," Bev said. "Just a little odd, maybe. Hey, I just wanted you to know I really liked your singing."

"Thanks, sugar. Doug's real sweet to let me sing here. I work the desk at his office, and one time I told him that I'd always wanted to be a singer, and he said, 'Poof! You're a singer then.' I ain't seen you 'round here before."

"No, I live in Morgan. I'm new there. Name's Bev." She was so drunk that getting out that much information felt like a major accomplishment.

Cricket came over, looking elated. "Bev, Wayne asked be to go home with him. I really wanna say yes, but I don't wanna leave you stranded here neither."

Rhonda broke in. "Bev can stay at my place if she wants to. You can come over and pick her up in the mornin'. Wayne knows where I live at."

Cricket looked at Bev questioningly. What the hell. She didn't know if Rhonda was propositioning her or not, but what if she was? It had been a long time since she had felt a woman in her arms. "Sure, Cricket. Just pick me up at Rhonda's in the morning."

"Bev, you are so great!" Cricket squealed. He kissed her on the cheek and then pranced back to Wayne.

"You don't care to spend the night at my house, do you?" Rhonda asked when he was gone.

"No, I don't care."

Rhonda's house turned out to be a trailer. "I

don't want you to get the wrong idea," Rhonda said, flipping on the light switch to reveal a living room filled with floral print furniture and knickknack shelf after knickknack shelf brimming with figurines of frolicking woodland creatures. "We don't have to do nothin'. I just wanted me some company, you know?"

"I know."

"There's some beers in the fridge. You want one?"

The last thing she needed was another beer, but she found herself saying sure anyway. Bev sat down on the overstuffed sofa and found herself looking at a framed photo on the end table. At first she thought it was a picture of a young, boyish-looking man, then she decided it was probably a young, boyish-looking woman. "Who's this in the picture?" she asked when Rhonda came into the living room with the beers.

"That's Sam — she's my sweetheart."

"Where is she?" Bev was suddenly paranoid.

"She's gone."

"Is she who you think about when you sing those songs?"

"Honey, she's who I think about all the time." She took the picture, looked at it a moment, then set it back on the table. "Stupid girl. She was always forgettin' she was a girl. That was what got her killed. Been treated like a boy so long she forgot she wasn't one."

"She's dead?" For some reason, Bev hadn't thought that "gone" meant *dead.*

"Got killed two year ago. Hit was the stupidest thing. She was drivin' her truck down one of them backroads one night, and it give out on her. I reckon she couldn't fix whatever was wrong with it, so she walked on down the road for help. A truckload of boys pulled over and told her to get in, so she did. Stupid. You know, she never thought she was differ'nt. She thought she was a boy just like they was, but they knowed she wasn't like them. The thing was, honey, she was better'n the whole carload of 'em. Maybe they knowed that, too. Maybe that's why they done . . . what they done."

Bev was crying along with Rhonda. She reached out and took her hand. "Jesus, Rhonda. Jesus, I'm sorry."

"Jesus," Rhonda repeated. "I ain't got much use for Jesus no more. Them boys got off easy. They went to jail for manslaughter. *Man*slaughter. Shoot, if she'd been a man, they wouldn'ta killed her. Sometimes I think when them boys gets out of jail, and they will get out, too, soon, me and my shotgun just might pay 'em a little visit."

"Rhonda, I don't know what to say."

"There ain't nothin to say. Besides, I know you been hurt, too. I seen you spillin' your heart out to that Stanley guy."

"It's nothing compared to you. I — I broke up with my girlfriend, is all."

"Honey, that's somethin'. At least with Sam dead and gone I don't have to get jealous thinkin' about her bein' with somebody else."

Bev thought of Andie playing it straight with Gary. She wondered if the game was still on.

Rhonda slapped Bev on the knee. "You know, for two drunk dykes, we're not havin' us a damn bit of fun. Like I said, you don't have to do nothin' you don't wanna do, but you wanna come back to the bed with me?"

Bev thought of how much Andie had hurt her,

and yet how her own pain was dwarfed by the magnitude of Rhonda's loss. Two women, each of them in pain, reaching out to each other. "Yeah," Bev said. "Yeah, okay."

They lay on the bed under a tapestry of dogs playing poker. Bev kissed Rhonda. It was the first time she had kissed a woman other than Andie in almost eight years. It felt alien, almost unnatural. When Bev pulled away, Rhonda said, "It ain't no good, is it?"

"No, it's fine. I'm just a little nervous is all."

"No," Rhonda said, sitting up. "It ain't no good for me neither. There ain't no sense for us to even try this what with us both bein' in love with somebody else."

It was true. "Look. I don't have anywhere else to go, so I'll just camp out on your couch, okay? You won't even know I'm here."

Rhonda touched her hand. "It's okay. Stay in the bed. We can just sleep."

They passed out in their clothes. Bev awoke to the beeping of Cricket's car horn outside. For a moment, she had absolutely no idea where she was and only a vague idea who she was. Rhonda was somehow managing to sleep through Cricket's incessant beeping. "Rhonda, Cricket's here. I've got to go," she said. Rhonda stirred slightly in her sleep, her face looking years older in the harsh sunlight that streamed in through the window. Bev leaned over and kissed her cheek. "Good-bye," she whispered.

Rhonda smiled with her eyes closed and reached up to touch the just-kissed spot on her face. "Sam," she sighed.

Bev regarded the morning sunlight with the enthusiasm of a vampire who had accidentally set the alarm clock for A.M. She opened the car door and collapsed into the passenger seat. "Jesus, you were a little enthusiastic with that car horn, weren't you?"

Cricket was aglow. The bright purple hickey on his neck was the exact same shade as his purple shirt.

"God," Bev said, "do you even color-coordinate your hickeys?"

Cricket laughed. "Somebody's grumpy this morning."

"Just hung over." Her head was pounding, and her tongue felt like a dry sponge. "I take it you had a good time?"

Cricket's little mouth stretched into an impossibly wide grin. "Bev, I'm in love!"

Chapter 17

Mamaw Needham was sweet to have invited Andie over for an early Thanksgiving dinner since, as she had put it, "You're so far away from your own people." Andie just wished that Gary didn't have to accompany her to this meal. But then again, she wished that Gary didn't have to accompany her anywhere. She had done everything she could think of to make him angry, to make him realize that they were about as ill-suited for each other as two people could be.

But still, it all continued — the rambling monologues he assumed she was interested in, the dinner dates, the intolerable scratchy-bearded good-night kisses. At least the fact that he was a fundamentalist Christian had kept him from initiating any more intimate contact. Gary believed in "saving himself" for marriage. Andie was thankful for that small favor, as long as he wasn't thinking that the marriage of which he spoke would involve her. Ugh. Did having a successful career have to mean giving up your will entirely?

Gary showed up at her door wearing a tie. He always wore a tie. She hated that. They were going to Mamaw Needham's, for Chrissakes. Ancil Needham had probably never worn a tie in his life unless he was going to a funeral. "Gee, I feel underdressed," Andie said, looking down at her jeans and sweater.

"You look lovely."

"Why don't we walk on over to Mamaw's?" She always tried to avoid inviting Gary into her house; he invaded her space enough as it was.

They walked across the lawn. Bo came sidling up to them, wagging his tail joyously. Andie leaned down to pet him, then noticed the extra car in Mamaw Needham's driveway. "I think that car belongs to Cricket. I didn't know he was joining us." The idea of Cricket's presence made Andie nervous since he was such good friends with Bev.

"Isn't he a mortician or something?"

"Nice guy, though," Andie said absently.

Mamaw Needham answered the door in the short-sleeved housedress and orthopedic sandals that she apparently wore regardless of season. "Well, you'uns come on in. Andie, this must be your feller."

"This is Gary Clark. Gary, Mamaw Needham."

“The Clarks over to the college,” Mamaw Needham said. “I know your people.”

“It’s a pleasure to meet you, Mrs. Needham.”

“Oh, honey, you just call me Mamaw.”

Ancil, whom Andie had laid eyes on only once before, was sitting in the La-Z-Boy recliner in the corner, staring at a game show on TV and ignoring the social buzz around him. His concentration seemed to be focused on chewing a huge wad of tobacco and spitting periodically into a JFG coffee can.

When she turned her attention away from Ancil, Andie saw a sight that made her wonder what she was going to do first: cry, faint, or throw up. Cricket was there, all right, but sitting beside him on Mamaw Needham’s atrocious pheasant-and-wagon-wheel print sofa was Bev. Andie was not sure what kind of expression was on her own face, but she suspected it was probably a mirror image of Bev’s: eyes wide, jaw slack, skin pale.

Mamaw Needham patted Andie on her stiffened shoulder. “I didn’t tell you I was gonna invite your cousin, did I? I didn’t tell her neither. I thought it’d be a nice surprise, a real family holiday.”

“You didn’t tell me you had a cousin here,” Gary said. “You said all your family was in Massachusetts.”

“Andie doesn’t like to talk about me, do you, Andie?” Bev’s voice was as icy as it had been the last time she’d spoken to her. “I’m sort of the bad girl of the family.”

“I don’t know about that, Bev,” Mamaw Needham said. “I think you’re just as sweet as you can be. And I know Cricket don’t think you’re bad. Do you, Cricket?”

Cricket was clearly trying to mentally remove

himself as far away from this situation as possible. "What? Oh. That's right, Mamaw Needham."

Ancil cackled at a commercial on the TV. "Them dogs," he laughed. "Them dogs with their little lunch buckets."

"So," Mamaw Needham said, "is ice tea all right with everbody?"

Mamaw had prepared a huge meal: fried chicken, mashed potatoes and gravy, pinto beans, biscuits, cooked apples, corn on the cob, and chicken and dumplings. Since there was no dining room, everybody crowded around the rectangular kitchen table, Andie and Gary on one side, Bev and Cricket on the other, and Mamaw and Ancil on either end. It was like some bizarre satire of *The Waltons.*

"So, Bev," Gary began. Andie could hardly swallow her piece of biscuit because her throat had constricted so tightly. "Are you Andie's first cousin?"

"Yes." Bev glared evilly at Andie. "I'm the illegitimate daughter of Andie's mother's younger sister. Nobody knows who my father is. Andie's aunt got around so much it was anybody's guess. Women in our family just go crazy when they get around men, don't they, Andie?"

Andie opened her mouth, but no sound would come out.

"Anyway," Bev continued in a hurt tone, "nobody knows who my daddy is. I guess that's why I don't come up much in family conversations."

Mamaw Needham pointed at Bev with a chicken leg. "Beverly, you can't help not knowin' who your daddy is. Children don't ask to be born into this world. Ain't that right, PAPAW NEEDHAM?" On *Papaw Needham,* her voice went up several decibels.

"What's that, Mamaw?" he said. Andie hadn't seen him remove the tobacco from his mouth before he started eating, and this bothered her.

"Bless his ol' heart. He's deaf as a post," Mamaw Needham muttered. "I SAID," she yelled so that anyone in Kentucky or any of the states adjoining it could hear, "CHILDREN DON'T ASK TO BE BORN INTO THIS WORLD, AIN'T THAT RIGHT, PAPAW NEEDHAM?"

"That's right, Mamaw," he mumbled, sopping up gravy with his biscuit.

"Poor ol' thing, couldn't hear it thunder," Mamaw Needham said.

"Mrs. Needham," Gary said, apparently unable to let the word *Mamaw* pass from his lips, "I believe these are the best chicken and dumplings I've ever eaten."

"Thank you, honey, but hit's squirrel."

"I beg your pardon?"

"Hit's squirrel and dumplin's." She stirred the huge pot of dumplings and ladled up a tiny rodent skull. "See, here's his little head," she said, pleased.

Papaw Needham started cackling again. Andie wasn't sure if he was laughing at the squirrel head or thinking again about the TV commercial that had so amused him. So far, the only positive thing to come out of this evening was that she had passed on the alleged chicken and dumplings.

Mamaw Needham dropped the skull back into the pot with a splash. "Reckon that taught the little booger to come into my yard and eat up all my birdseed!" she laughed. "Why, I seen him out there, and I just took my shotgun, and —"

"Mamaw, you're just awful," Cricket interrupted.

"You shouldn't talk about shootin' things at the dinner table. It's not appetizin'."

"You're probly right," Mamaw Needham said. "Say, did they bring anybody into the funeral home today?"

"They brung in Old Man Siler. He had a heart attack, you know. He was hard to fix up, let me tell you. His eyes had bugged out of his head, and his face was just as blue as that sweater Andie's got on."

Andie looked down at her sweater in horror.

By the time they got around to the blackberry cobbler, Andie was certain that she had fallen into some kind of black hole where time expanded. How long had this meal taken? Six hours? Three days? As she sat here drinking iced tea so heavily sweetened that it slithered down her throat like molasses, Gary was holding her hand under the table. She knew that Bev knew what Gary was doing. She knew that Bev thought she was a liar and a hypocrite. And the worst part was that Bev was right.

Andie and Gary excused themselves soon after dessert. As they made their way back to the house, Gary said, "I can't believe I ate squirrel. But I had already said it was good, so I couldn't very well stop eating it just because I knew what it was."

Andie didn't say anything. She didn't want to chitchat. She wanted to dump Gary, lock herself into her house, and never come out again.

"You don't like your cousin much, do you?"

God, he was such an idiot. "It's really complicated, and you don't know anything about it, okay?"

"I wouldn't say that. I have an awfully good sense about people. And while I don't understand why you kept Beverly a secret from me, I do understand why you dislike her. She's almost the complete opposite of you, so bitter and abrasive. Why, there's almost something masculine about her."

"Gary, I don't want to talk about Bev, okay?"

"Okay, okay. But you have to admit that she and Cricket make an odd couple. If they are a couple. He seems a little light in the loafers, don't you think?"

She could put up with his off-key singing in church. She could even suffer through his deer hunting stories. But she could not stand here and put up with his homophobic comments about Cricket and the woman with whom she had shared seven years of her life. She wheeled around to face him. "Gary, you are such an idiot. You think you have everything figured out. Well, you know nothing. You know nothing about the world, you know nothing about human relationships, and you sure as hell know nothing about me!"

She broke into a full run and unlocked the front door while Gary stood in the spot where she had left him, pleading ineffectually, "Andie, wait." She locked the door behind her and ran straight to the back room, where she flung herself into bed and pulled the covers over her head. She buried her face in a pillow until the inevitable knocking at the door stopped.

Though her eyes were closed, she kept seeing Bev sitting on that ugly pheasant-and-wagon-wheel couch next to Cricket. Bev, wearing that white tuxedo blouse Andie had seen her in hundreds of times. Bev, whose body Andie knew as well as she knew her own. That one moment that Andie had looked at Bev before Bev had seen her, she had been so cool, so self-possessed, so much the Bev she had always loved.

But then when Bev had seen her, her eyes had held nothing for Andie but contempt. And why should she not be contemptuous? Seeing Andie there with Gary only confirmed everything she had said on the night she walked out.

Maybe her blow-up at Gary had at least gotten rid of him, Andie hoped as kitty lang crawled under the covers to join her. Even if Bev hated her, she at least could take some comfort in not having to feign a heterosexual relationship. Better to be a real spinster schoolteacher than a fake heterosexual. Kitty lang rubbed up against her, purring. "Oh, kitty," Andie sighed. "I miss your other mommy."

As the sunlight streamed in through the bedroom window, Andie was awakened by a knock at the door. She had no recollection of having fallen asleep and had no concept of what time it might be. Groggy and still wearing last night's clothes, she staggered into the living room and opened the door. It was a young, pimply-faced man whom she didn't recognize.

"You Andrea Pritchard?"

"Yes?"

"Flowers for you, ma'am." He shoved a bud vase of two red roses at her.

"Oh . . . thanks." She closed the door, set down the vase, and opened the card. On it was scrawled, "My heartfelt apologies, Gary."

She wadded up the card and hurled it across the room. "Shit!" There was nothing else to say. "Shit, shit, shit."

Chapter 18

"Uh-huh," Bev was saying for the hundredth time. She was on the phone with Cricket, listening to him declare and redeclare his love for Wayne.

"It's hilarious," Cricket said. "Nobody even suspects that he's my boyfriend. He come down here last night, and we ran smack into Daddy at the funeral home. I was just so scared I didn't know what to do, but Daddy was real polite to him, and Wayne, well, he's always just as sweet as he can be. Then today at work Daddy kinda took me aside and said, Son, I like that Wayne boy. It's good to see you keepin' company with some real men for a change." Cricket whooped with laughter. "I reckon he thinks Wayne's gonna be a good influence on me!"

"I'm really happy for you, Cricket." It wasn't exactly the truth, but she was trying her best to be happy for him. It was just so hard to see him and Wayne so consumed with love for each other while the woman she still loved was having a sham romance with a rat-toothed, buttoned-down, male history professor.

"Of course, it is kinda hard right now, what with him livin' in Odessa and me in Morgan. We pretty much have to see each other just on the weekends. But come next fall, he's startin' school part-time at that new community college they're buildin' over in Taylorsville, so then he'll be passin' through town a couple a times a week. He says he always wanted to go to college, but 'til now, he never had the time or the money. I'm kickin in a little of the money. Course, he didn't ask me to or nothin'. Do you think that's okay?"

"Huh? Oh. Sure." She was trying to concentrate on what he was saying, but since the other night at Mamaw Needham's, she had not been able to think of much except Andie, Andie sitting there beside Gary like she was his personal property, like what they had was real.

"Part of the reason Wayne ain't never been to college is because he says he wouldn't go to Randall for a million dollars. He said he was even worried about goin' to that new community college and bein' gay, but then he met the fella that's gonna be dean there at The Hideaway. Says he's queer as a three-dollar bill. But anyway, Wayne wants to be a nurse, and I'm thinkin' that maybe when he gets his degree I could maybe get him a job over here at Farmer Memorial. Then we could both be in the same town. Wouldn't that just be perfect?"

"Yeah. Look, Cricket, I gotta go. It's almost time for my class to start."

"Okay, hon. But listen, try to cheer up a little, okay? It's the holiday season."

"Don't remind me."

As much as she would have liked to, forgetting about the holidays didn't seem to be an option. Red plastic bells hung from the streetlights in Morgan, and an equally synthetic nativity set was on display in front of the courthouse, separation of church and state be damned. Every structure that could possibly be outlined in garish, multicolored lights had been: houses, trailers, toolsheds, satellite dishes.

When she had wandered through the few local stores looking for presents for next week's obligatory holiday visit home, the ubiquitous Christmas Muzak had pounded in her brain until she had to go back to her apartment, take two aspirin, and lie down. No doubt about it, people in Morgan took the celebration of Christmas seriously, as was evidenced by the fact that the students in her nutrition and childcare class had insisted that tonight's meeting, their final one, take the form of a Christmas party.

Bev walked into the center to find her students and their guests already there: Tammy and Wanda; Lisa and a girl who looked like a younger sister; and

Charlene and her three little boys, who were gleefully chasing each other up and down the aisles of the thrift store. Teresa and Michelle were there, too, since as Wanda had put it, "I reckon it'd be rude not to invite 'em."

"Hey, everybody," Bev said, trying to sound cheerful. She set a box of Christmas cookies down on the table in the Kaffeeklatsch Korner, and Charlene's children soon descended on the food like starving POWs.

"Now, young'uns," Charlene cautioned. "No more'n three cookies apiece." She shook her head and grinned at Bev. "They're the craziest things about cookies you ever seen." She patted her tummy thoughtfully. "After three boys, I sure hope this'un's a girl."

Bev felt a hand on her shoulder. It was Teresa.

"You've done a wonderful job with these women," she said. "Not only have you educated them, but by bringing them together, you've provided them with an important feminine support network."

Bev looked around the room. Tammy and Lisa were laughing, comparing the sizes of each other's tummies. Wanda and Charlene were talking about baby names. Jeanie, the one student who wasn't present, had come by the other day to tell Bev that she had moved in with her aunt and was going back to high school. For once, Bev had to agree with Teresa. She had done a good job. Her personal life was in shambles, but at least she had this to feel good about. Moving to Kentucky hadn't been a total waste after all.

"Okay, present time," she announced. She grabbed

Charlene's oldest boy by his sticky-with-icing hand. "What's your name?"

"Hershel."

Poor kid, Bev thought. "Hershel, would you like to play Santa and help me hand out presents?"

A shipment of baby clothes had come into the shop a couple of weeks ago, and Bev had purchased the best of them, so that each of her students would receive a gift package of six sets of baby clothes.

"Bev, you shouldn't have bought us all this stuff. You're our teacher," Lisa said.

"It's no big deal. It's stuff that came into the store."

"Me and the girls chipped in on a little somethin' for you," Wanda said. "Tammy, you wanna give it to her?"

Tammy presented Bev with a small white box. "It's nothin' much," she said.

Bev opened the box to find a tiny silver cross pendant on a thin silver chain. She hadn't worn a cross since she was in Catholic school.

"You really shouldn't have . . ." It was all she could think of to say. The women were poor; they didn't need to be buying her gifts.

"Hit's just silver plated, so don't think we went and spent a lot of money," Tammy said.

Lisa slapped Tammy gently on the back. "Girl, don't you know you ain't supposed to tell people you didn't spend a lot of money on 'em?"

Tammy grinned. "Okay, we spent a lot of money on it, then. Me and Lisa picked it out. We thought it was real pretty."

"It's beautiful," Bev said, turning around so

Tammy could fasten the clasp. The pendant hung just below the hollow of her neck, and it was beautiful, not in and of itself, maybe, but because of the women who gave it to her. She held the tiny pendant between her thumb and forefinger. "I'll never take it off."

Chapter 19

Kitty lang dashed into the living room and leapt right into the middle of Eugenia Randall's papers. "Kitty, stop it!" Andie fussed. "These are important papers." They were supposed to be important papers anyway, but so far kitty lang had found a more worthwhile use for them than she had. So far as she could tell, there wasn't a single thing of interest in the whole boxload of them. She had found dull letters from Eugenia's family members ("We're so proud that you have set out to do God's work in the mountains") and notes Eugenia had written to herself

("Must look into requiring full medical examinations for all incoming students"). Last night she had gotten so bored that she had fallen asleep facedown in the box of papers, dozing there until she started sneezing from all the dust.

But now she had to get serious. She had resolved to spend all of her winter break hard at work on the Randall papers. To hell with the holidays; she couldn't force herself to be festive anyway. Thankfully, Gary was going to be on vacation with his parents for most of the break, so she wouldn't have to fake any holiday cheer around him. She had sent a poinsettia to her parents's house in Boston so she wouldn't seem like a total Scrooge. Now she could just be left alone — an old maid schoolteacher spending the holiday season with her cat and a stack of yellowed papers.

She wondered if Bev would be going back to Boston for Christmas, or back to Boston indefinitely. She had nothing to keep her here. Stop it, concentrate on the papers, she told herself. She picked up a piece of paper on which a poem had been neatly printed:

When I look up at the mountains, then I can truly see
The glory and the splendor of God's great plan for me.
It is in the eyes of children, too, this marvelous plan,
For to feed and school them with love is my Lord's command.
And every night I ask my Lord upon my bended knee

To give me strength to fulfill my holy destiny.
—E. Randall

Ugh. Andie fervently hoped that her task here was not to analyze Eugenia Randall's contribution to literature. The problem she was having with Randall so far was that while she was without a doubt a good person, dedicated to helping those in need and founding the school that would later become Randall College, she was not a particularly interesting person. It was almost as if she were too good, too pure of heart, for Andie (or, she hoped, for any normal, run-of-the-mill person) to be able to identify with her. Andie began to wonder if Eugenia Randall had ever taken enough time out from her mission to pee or get laid. Probably not, Andie decided, wading through the papers to get a soda from the fridge. Getting laid would have been sinful, and peeing would probably have been considered unladylike.

Can of soda in hand, Andie plopped back down in the middle of the papers. Her attention was suddenly caught by an envelope with a return address that read, "Mildred Farmer, Rural Nurses Summer Training Program, Tandy Creek, Kentucky." A nurse. Wasn't the local hospital called Farmer Memorial? She pulled the letter out of the envelope and read:

My dearest Eugenia:

The days pass slowly here without you, though the work is, as always, rewarding. The new girls here are bright and enthusiastic. One particularly bright-eyed girl from back in the hills asked me on her first day, "When do I get to birth a baby?" I told her there was much to learn about midwifery before she would actually be allowed to "birth" a baby. And I was right in saying so. Yesterday, I took her and another girl to watch me assist a breech birth, and both of the girls grew faint at the sight of the blood! They were very apologetic afterwards; I told them they would grow used to it in time.

How is your work at school? I do hope that you are not working yourself too hard. I know you better than anyone, my darling, and I know that without me there to take care of you, you will work yourself past the point of exhaustion. When I return to Morgan next month, I want to see you well-fed and well-rested.

Oh, my dear Eugenia, if the days here are long, then the nights are endless. I lie in my hard, narrow cot dreaming of our nights together in your luxuriantly soft feather bed, of the sweetness of you in my arms, of the perfume of your hair, of my head resting safe against your soft bosom. Oh, how I long to touch you again! I know that it is not proper for women to speak of such things, but your love acts on me like a potion which brings forth the truth. With you, I must speak freely.

I know that every minute that ticks away brings me closer to that blessed time when I can hold you again, and so I remain your loving,

Mildred

Andie scanned back through the letter to make

sure she had read it correctly. It was all there, all right: the endless nights, the perfumed hair, the soft bosom. Was she right to assume on the basis of this letter that Eugenia Randall was involved in what was at least a highly homoerotic relationship? Jesus, what else could she assume?

She rifled through the papers with new enthusiasm, searching desperately for more letters to Eugenia from Mildred. There were letters from Eugenia's mother, from her sister in Philadelphia, and from former students who had gone on to become successful teachers themselves, but no more letters from Mildred. Andie looked again at the return address on Mildred's envelope: "Rural Nurses Summer Training Program." Perhaps that summer was the only time she had been separated from Eugenia. Mildred apparently lived in Morgan as well, given her references in the letter and given the fact that the local hospital bore her name.

The two women could have shared a daily life together, doing good in the community by day and coming home to each other at night. That was wonderful for them, of course, but it did create a problem for Andie in that a daily life together didn't produce the same sort of documents that a long-distance relationship did. Andie needed more letters, needed anything tangible that could document that the women had a relationship. But there were no more letters, no more anything.

On a whim, Andie picked up a worn, slim book that was sitting in the bottom of the box. It was the only book in the collection, and Andie wondered how it had found its way into this assortment of unconnected papers. She opened the book and saw that it was Elizabeth Barrett Browning's *Sonnets from the Portuguese*. On the blank page preceding the poems was a handwritten inscription:

To Eugenia on her birthday —
Let me count the ways,
Mildred

So it was true. These two exceptional women had lived together and worked together and loved together right here in Morgan, and in the process of building a pedestal for them, history had also built a closet around them. Jesus, what was she going to say when she made her presentation? Was she going to bury the only enlightening thing she found in the papers and give a safe little public reading of the inane poetry of Eugenia Randall? What kind of bizarre cosmic joke was this? She had, however unintentionally, sacrificed the love of her life in order to be a safely closeted Randall faculty member, and now she had to decide whether or not to keep Eugenia Randall herself safely in the closet.

In bed that night, Andie's sleeping mind turned to the Morgan, Kentucky, of years past. In the dream, she was Eugenia Randall. Her heavy skirts dragged the floor, and the whalebone corset beneath her blouse cut into her ribs. A woman, also dressed in a long skirt, held out her hand to Eugenia/Andie. Andie gave the woman her hand and let her lead her down a long, dark hallway that led to a white bedroom flooded with light. The woman pushed Eugenia/Andie down on the large, soft bed and began slowly, meticulously, undoing the dozens of tiny buttons on her blouse. The clothing came off layer by layer;

Eugenia/Andie was being peeled like an onion, down to the core. The blouse, the skirts, the petticoats, the corset, the stockings, the pantalets, layer by layer by layer. The woman then tore off her own constricting clothing as roughly and as quickly as possible so that when she pressed against Eugenia/Andie, soft, liberated flesh met soft, liberated flesh. "Mildred," Eugenia/Andie sighed, reaching up to loosen the woman's long, chestnut hair. "Oh, Mildred." But when she looked up at her dream lover, the face she saw was Bev's.

A strange ringing noise penetrated Andie's dream. The phone had rung a full four times before she was awake enough to figure out what it was. Groggy, she rolled over, picked up the receiver, and without thinking croaked, "Bev?"

"Were you expecting a call from your cousin?" It was Gary. Her dream was definitely over.

"No, I was sleeping. What time is it?"

"It just turned midnight, and you know what that means."

"No, not really." Andie wished that it meant Gary would turn into a pumpkin.

"It's December 25. I wanted to be the first person to wish you a merry Christmas."

"Oh. Merry Christmas to you, too." Her voice lacked conviction, but she didn't care. She hung up the phone and lay back down. Then she closed her eyes and tried to make her dream come back.

Chapter 20

Bev had decided that her trip home for Christmas should be as quick and efficient as possible. Teresa had told her that she was welcome to take a whole week off to spend time with friends and family, but to Bev, three days with her devoutly Catholic parents sounded quite sufficient, thank you. And while she had debated calling up some old friends in Boston, she just couldn't bring herself to pick up the phone. All of her old friends were also Andie's friends — couples whom Bev and Andie had socialized with together. Calling everybody and confessing her solitary state would make people click their tongues and say, "I knew that move to Kentucky was a terrible idea."

And so there she was, in her parents' house, wide-eyed and sleepless in the bed of her adolescence, reminding herself that all she had to do was survive tomorrow and then she could get on a plane first thing the next morning, and Cricket would be waiting for her at the airport in Lexington. But then what? Then, she would go back to Morgan to her dismal, empty apartment.

Funny how being in your old room reduces you to a teenage level, she thought. She never really felt like an adult when she visited her parents. How could she? Lying under the pink frilly bedspread she had always hated and staring at her high school field-hockey trophies reduced her to her most insecure core of identity, the tomboy who had never fit in.

The door opened a crack, letting a shaft of light from the hallway into the room. "Bev," a voice whispered, "you up?"

"Yeah."

"Good." Her younger sister Maureen, wearing a silky gown and robe that looked like they had been purchased in one of those mall lingerie stores, tiptoed into the room, "Couldn't get to sleep after midnight mass, huh?"

"Nope."

"Me either. I could barely get the kids to bed. I finally told them there was no way in hell Santa would come if they didn't go to sleep. It's a mean mommy trick. I've got a million of 'em." She fished a pack of cigarettes out of the pocket of her robe. "You still smoke?"

"I've officially quit two times since last Christmas, but yes."

"Good. I know Mom wants us to go outside, but goddamn it, if I'm gonna give myself cancer I wanna do it where it's nice and warm."

"Shut the door," Bev said, sitting up and retrieving her cigarettes from the nightstand. "We can sneaks cigs in here like bad girls."

Maureen smiled. "Yep, blow the smoke out the window like we did when we were teenagers." She cracked the window, lit a cigarette, and blew a stream of smoke outside. "Say, do you remember when Sister Mary Immaculate caught me with that pack of Camel cigarettes and made me scrub the floor of the girls' room with a toothbrush?"

"She was one tough nun."

"She liked you, though. All the nuns hated me. I was too boy crazy. And of course, you weren't boy crazy at all, so they assumed you were going to grow up and be a nun, too."

Bev laughed. "Little did they know."

Maureen reached over and patted Bev on the knee. "We both turned out to be bad girls. Between your tragic sexual orientation, and my nasty little divorce, I'm sure Mom wonders where she went wrong."

"Not a priest or a nun in the whole nuclear family."

"I can't help noticing that cross you're wearing. You're not going back to your roots, are you, sis?"

Bev fingered the silver pendant. "No. My students gave it to me — in that nutrition and childcare class

I taught. I wear it because of them." She stared out the window at the line of non-descript houses that dotted the street. When she had been in Catholic school, she had delighted in the fact that the nuns loved her. She would flush with pleasure when old Sister Martha would ask her to erase the board or when young, athletic Sister Theresa would slap her on the back after a particularly good field-hockey game. At the time, she had really wanted to be a nun. Now she realized that her desire was probably an early manifestation of her desire to spend her life in the company of other women.

Or was it? After all, now she was living a celibate life in rural Appalachia, helping poor and underprivileged women. She even wore a cross around her neck. She wasn't a practicing Catholic anymore, but it was a little scary how in the past few months her life had moved from one form of sisterhood to another. Was it possible to be a secular nun?

"Bev?"

Her mind snapped back to the immediate present. "Huh?"

"You zoned out on me, sis. That was the third time I said your name."

"Sorry."

"What are you thinking about?"

"Nothing, really." Maureen was Bev's favorite sibling, but that didn't mean that she was comfortable discussing her personal problems with her. In her family, Bev had always functioned as a listener, not a talker. It was safer that way.

"Come on, Bev. You think I haven't noticed how

broody you are? I know the whole family Christmas thing drives you nuts, but it's more than that, isn't it?"

"Maybe."

"No maybes about it. Look, I know you don't like to talk about your personal life with Mom and Dad around, but it's just you and me now. So, how have things been going with your girlfriend since she dragged you to Bumfuck, Egypt?"

She could have said okay, but something stopped her. "I don't have a girlfriend anymore."

"I guess that answers my question. Jesus, you and Andie were together for —"

"Seven years."

"Seven years! Wow, that's like . . . a divorce."

That's exactly what it was like, and yet Bev was a little surprised to hear Maureen equate her and Andie's breakup to her own failed marriage. "Yeah."

"Hell, you were together longer than Richard and me. Was it the move that did it?"

"That and a lot of things. Mainly Andie wanting to keep our relationship a big secret for career reasons, and being willing to date a man to do it."

"No way!"

"Yep."

"God, that's so weird! Richard and I just split because we didn't get along. It's weird to think about breaking up because of the fear that just being in the relationship you're in could make you lose your job." She lit another cigarette. "It's weird for me to think about anyway."

"Of course it is. You're straight."

"Yeah. Are you pretty much stuck in . . . What's the name of the town again?"

"Morgan." She hadn't really thought of the question. "What do you mean?"

"I mean are you going back there?"

"I have to. There's my job, and all my stuff's there."

"Are you going back there for good? It seems to me if the only reason you moved to that godforsaken place is because of Andie, now that you've broken up with her, you don't really have any reason to be there anymore."

"I don't know if I have any other options."

"Of course you do! Come back to Boston. Stay at my place 'til you find an apartment — or stay at my place indefinitely, for all I care. I got the house out of the divorce; there's plenty of room. The kids love you. And I've got a good job. I could even carry you for a while until you find work, as long as you'd be willing to help out around the house."

Bev was overwhelmed by the generosity of her sister's offer. "Mo, I don't know what to say."

"Yes would be good."

"I couldn't impose on you."

"You wouldn't be imposing. The only thing I really miss about marriage is having a grownup to talk to when I get home from work. And believe me, you're much better company than Richard. Besides, Bev, you're a town girl like I am. You'd love to be back in the city."

"I'll have to think about it."

Maureen stood and retied her robe around her

waist. "Okay. Sleep on it, and let me know tomorrow. But promise me you won't say no just because you feel like you'd be taking advantage of me. I wouldn't make the invitation if I didn't mean it. I'm not that nice of a person. Promise?"

"Promise." Bev rose and hugged Maureen tightly. "Thanks, sis."

Maureen broke away and patted Bev on the cheek. "Don't mention it. Now get in bed and go to sleep, or Santa won't come."

No doubt about it, Bev loved the city — its open and active gay and lesbian community, not to mention the cultural attractions: the theaters, the museums, the bookstores, the restaurants. She had been happy in Boston. She had been happy there with Andie. But it was hard to imagine being happy there without her.

Back in Morgan, there were Cricket and Wayne and Tammy and Wanda and Mamaw Needham. There was the Mountain Women's Outreach Center, where she had to admit she loved her work. Even if Teresa was somewhat annoying, Bev's annoyance was overshadowed by the satisfaction of being able to help women like Jeanie. Her personal life was miserable, but no matter where she went, her personal life would be miserable because she didn't have Andie. Hell, maybe she was supposed to have been a nun all along.

As a little girl, Bev had loved *The Wizard of Oz*, but she had never understood why Dorothy would choose the barren black-and-white Kansas landscape over the vibrant Technicolor Emerald City. But now, as she lay in bed, thinking Boston or Morgan,

Morgan or Boston, over and over again, she suddenly understood Dorothy's decision. There's no place like home, she thought. She had lost her lover, but she still had a home. She was going back to Morgan.

Chapter 21

"Needham and Son's Family Funeral Home," the secretary's voice droned on the other end of the line.

Andie took a gulp of beer for courage.

"Hello? Needham and Son's."

"Yes, hello," Andie heard herself saying. "I'd like to speak to Cricket Needham, please."

"I'll have to see if he's available. Please hold."

Andie heard the secretary push a button and then was forced to listen to the entirety of "Mamas, Don't

Let Your Babies Grow Up to Be Cowboys." Another country ditty was beginning when Cricket finally answered.

"Hi, this is Cricket!" His tone seemed a little perky for someone answering the phone at a funeral home.

"Cricket, this is Andie Pritchard."

"Oh . . . Bev's cousin?" he asked, Andie thought, with a hint of irony.

Andie sighed. These small-town people certainly had a higher tolerance for keeping up appearances than she did. "Look, Cricket. You hang out with Bev all the time, so you have to know what the deal is." She paused, hoping Cricket would say something. He didn't. Okay, so she'd say it. "You know Bev and I were lovers, right?"

"I know that. Honey, I don't mean to be rude, but I'm up to my elbows in embalming fluid here, and I need to know what you're gettin' at."

Andie worked hard not to picture Cricket standing over a gutted corpse. She had to get to the point. She was always telling her students to be clear and concise. Now was the time to practice what she preached. "Okay. First of all, I need to ask you a question. Is Bev still in town?"

"She went home for Christmas, but she's back now."

"Okay, good. I feel weird asking you for a favor, Cricket, because I figure that Bev's probably told you that I'm the bitch of the century."

"Bev's never said nothin' like that about you."

"Really? Well, the thing is, Cricket, on Friday,

January tenth, at eight P.M., I'm giving a presentation in the auditorium at Randall. What I need you to do is make sure that Bev is there."

"And how am I supposed to do that?"

"Any way you can. Lie to her. Drag her there. Do whatever works."

"Andie, why are you askin' me to do this?"

"Because she wouldn't come if I asked her to. She probably wouldn't even come if she knew I was going to be there."

"But I don't understand —"

"Look, it'll all be clear when you get there. If you don't want to do this for me, I'll understand. But if you do this for me, Cricket, well . . . it might just be the nicest thing anyone has ever done for me."

"Andie?"

"Yes?"

"Is Bev gonna hate me for this?"

"I hope not, Cricket. I hope not."

The auditorium wasn't exactly packed. There was a scattering of students, a few of whom were in Andie's composition classes. Gary was in the front row, beaming like a proud boyfriend. Dean Clark and President Malcolm sat reared back in the second row, puffed up with institutional pride. The rest of the second row was filled with English department folk. Hill was there with Bobby and Payne and Nina, who was accompanied by Inez. Joyce and her already snoozing mother were in the fifth row. Other than that, the audience seemed to be made up of a few faculty and staff people Andie only vaguely recognized. Maybe Cricket hadn't been able to persuade Bev to come. Or maybe he just hadn't tried.

But then, as Andie stepped up to the podium, they shuffled in: Cricket followed by Bev followed by an enormous bearded man in a plaid flannel shirt. They slid into the back row without looking toward the head of the room. But once Bev was seated, she looked up. Andie's eyes locked with hers across the auditorium. Bev broke the gaze and jumped out of her seat to escape, but Cricket grabbed her gently by the arm, and the formidable bearded man stood and blocked her exit. Defeated, she sank back into her chair.

Andie looked down at the notes she clutched in her quivering hands. Bev obviously hated her, so why was she even doing this? She looked around the auditorium. Everyone was staring at her, waiting. She had two options: talk or run. Since at the moment the options seemed roughly equivalent to choosing between death by hanging or death by firing squad, she decided to talk. What the hell. She could talk faster than she could run. Besides, maybe Bev wasn't the only person she was doing this for.

"G-good evening, and welcome to this presentation in honor of Eugenia Randall's birthday. I had never heard of Eugenia Randall until I came to Randall College for a job interview this past summer. Since that time, I have learned a great deal about Eugenia Randall's life and her work, which was one of the things she most valued. The more I have discovered about her, the more I have become convinced that she is yet another important female that the male-dominated field of history had erased from its pages. Eugenia Randall did at least as much for the rural poor as the more famous Jane Addams did for the urban poor. And while Addams's venerable Hull House is no longer in operation, Randall College still thrives, continuing to this day to carry out Eugenia Randall's mission: to bring education and opportunity to the mountains of Kentucky. As we sit here in this auditorium, all of us, students, faculty and staff, administrators, and Morgan community members, are part of Eugenia Randall's proud legacy."

She paused, took a breath. Though she didn't dare look at Bev, all the other audience members were gazing at her approvingly. So far, so good.

"But I didn't come here to talk about the history of Randall College; that subject would fare much better in the hands of an institutional historian. I came here to discuss Eugenia Randall, the woman. Dr. Hill asked me to prepare this presentation with the knowledge that my doctoral dissertation was on the subject of Women's Life Writing. One of my primary interests as a scholar is how women through the ages — often women who would never consider themselves writers in the traditional sense — reveal things about themselves and the times in which they lived through their own personal "scribblings," as they might self-deprecatingly call them. Women's letters, journal entries, poems written for personal enjoyment only, all of these can do much to break the silence of history. When I was given a box of Eugenia Randall's previously unexamined papers, I approached them as a scholar in the field of Women's Life Writing. And tonight, I would like to share and discuss some of Randall's life writing with you."

She read some of Randall's poems, trying not to make them sound as trite and singsongy as they actually were. She emphasized that the poems' literary merit (which was questionable) was not the issue; the important thing was what the poems said about Randall's values and feelings. She read some letters to Eugenia Randall from her mother, in which she expressed pride in her daughter's good deeds, but fear that her daughter would die a childless old maid. The audience was rapt, fascinated. Now was the time. Andie clutched the sides of the podium for support.

"It is interesting," she began, "that in the little writing that has been done on Eugenia Randall's life that no one ever mentions her personal life, her home life. She is painted as a tirelessly working, noble, solitary woman, a self-designed Protestant nun of sorts. No evidence is ever given that she was anything other than the old maid that her mother feared she was. And yet, the most fascinating piece of evidence I found in the papers indicates that Eugenia Randall did have a love in her life other than her work."

She had to concentrate to keep her voice from quavering as she read the love letter from Mildred Farmer, straight from the "My dearest Eugenia" to the "I remain your loving, Mildred," without leaving out a single reference to perfumed hair, soft beds, or soft bosoms.

Usually, in an auditorium filled with people, there is a constant low level of noise — throats being cleared, buttocks shifting in squeaky seats, the occasional cough or sneeze. But as Andie concluded the letter, the auditorium was as silent as a sealed vault. She could hear only the deafening bass drum beat of her heart and the thrumming of the blood in her veins. And all she could see was Bev in the last row staring straight at her, wondering what the hell she was going to do next.

Andie was not entirely sure what she was going to do next herself. She hadn't really planned her lecture beyond reading the letter, perhaps because she feared or hoped that she would be stricken dead in the process. As she stood before the mute audience, she was no longer Dr. Andrea Pritchard, the scholar and teacher. Now she was just plain Andie, and she was scared out of her wits.

"So you can see that history's attempt to cover up the love of Eugenia Randall's life is another example of how society attempts to desexualize women, particularly unmarried women. During Randall's lifetime, an unmarried woman was considered a sexless spinster, and today we haven't done much to change this part of Eugenia Randall's image. Why? Is it because the love of Randall's life was another woman, and the idea of the founder of a Christian institution being a lesbian — even if Randall didn't have access to that word — is just too unsavory?"

At this point, the silence in the auditorium was broken as President Malcolm stormed out, pursued by Dr. Hill and Dean Clark, who were on his heels like Chihuahuas trying to keep up with an English bulldog. Andie silently bid her job good-bye. She might as well go ahead and say her piece now. She had nothing to lose.

"And why should we find these two women who loved each other unsavory? After all, it was Eugenia Randall who brought higher education to this area and Mildred Farmer who brought modern health care to the region. They were good, devoutly Christian women who happened to love each other. And yet, until this moment, that fact has remained hidden in a box in a basement gathering dust. As is the case with so many other figures who happened to be gay, history has built a closet around Eugenia Randall and Mildred Farmer."

She looked past all the other slack-jawed audience members and straight at Bev. "Some of us don't have to wait for history to build a closet around us. When I took this job, I moved to Morgan with the only person I've ever loved, the only woman I've ever loved. But I didn't want to lose my job, so I started out telling everybody she was my cousin. That was the first lie, the first of many. As a matter of fact, before I even knew what hit me, I had built lie upon lie upon lie until I had built a closet around myself, a closet made of lies. There wasn't room in that closet for anybody but me."

Andie took a breath, amazed that no one was throwing stones at her yet. Better wind up fast. "You can imagine how I felt when I discovered that the college where I was so carefully closeting myself in order to keep my job was founded by a dyke! Anyway, I felt that I owed it to myself and to Bev and to all of you and to the memory of Eugenia Randall to tell the truth. Thank you."

There was really no need to say thank you because there was no applause. All Andie knew was that she had to get to Bev, but in order to do that she would have to walk across an auditorium populated with a number of people who could be in tough competition for the title of the Last Person on Earth She Wanted to Deal With Right Now. The first person she ran into as she stepped down from the stage was without a doubt the winner of the hypothetical contest.

"Gary, I guess 'I'm sorry' is hardly sufficient." His face was flushed with what was either extreme anger or extreme embarrassment.

"I will pray to the Lord to give me the strength to forgive you, Andrea. And I will pray that you, too, can find the Lord and turn from your sinning ways." His next words left little doubt as to the anger versus embarrassment question. "But first I'm gonna go talk to my daddy."

"You do that." She walked on toward the back of the room. She hadn't noticed that the auditorium was so big before. She felt sure that people had crossed entire deserts in less time than it was taking her to get from the stage to the back row. She saw that Nina was crying and that Inez was comforting her.

"She seemed like such a nice gull," Nina sobbed. "It's tragic. That's what it is. Simply tragic. Why, Inez, you don't think she thought we wuh —" She collapsed into hysterical sobbing.

"Hush yoah cryin', Nina!" Inez barked. "Nobody would evuh think that."

As she walked on down the aisle, Andie saw that Joyce's mother was, for the first time in Andie's memory, awake. "Joyce! Joyce!" she was screeching. "If you don't leave home and get married, people'll think you're like that filthy girl who was talkin' up there!"

"Shut up, Mother."

Suddenly Bobby was standing before her. Andie

didn't know what to say. She had considered Bobby a friend and wanted to be able to continue to do so.

Bobby draped his arm around her and patted her on the back. "They're gonna give you the axe for this, you know."

"I know."

"I'm gonna miss workin' with you, buddy."

She squeezed his hand. "You, too, Bobby. I'll keep in touch."

Eons later, she arrived at the back row. She realized now that her cheeks were wet because tears were streaming down her face. She wasn't sure how long she'd been crying.

Bev elbowed the two men on either side of her. "Cricket and Wayne told me we were coming to see the Randall College Film Club's showing of *All About Eve*. Sneaky bastards."

Andie wiped away tears. "Randall doesn't even have a film club." Cricket handed her a hanky. "Bev. I'm sorry for everything. I understand if you won't take me back. I don't know if I'd take me back either. I wanted to do this to show you and to show me that being with you and being honest with myself is more important than having a job."

Bev reached for Andie's hand. "C'mere." Andie opened her arms and crushed herself against her lover's body, thinking of all the nights she had awakened to find it was only a pillow she was hugging and not Bev.

Cricket tapped Andie on the shoulder. "Girls, this is so sweet I'm about to cry, but don't you think you might better kiss and make up somewhere else?"

"Yeah," Wayne added, herding them out of the auditorium, "I reckon you'uns better be takin' off before they get out the tar and feathers."

When they were outside, Cricket took Wayne's hand. "You girls have fun now."

"I have a feeling we will," Bev said, draping her arm around Andie. "Where are we going, Proud Out Dyke?"

Andie laughed. "Why don't we go back to our house?"

"Our house. That sounds good."

In the car, Andie said, "What are we going to do now?"

"That's easy. We're going home, and I'm going to do unmentionable things to your person."

"I don't mean this-minute now. I mean long-term now. I made the last big decision about our lives, and it was a disaster. I'm obviously out of work now, and I'm just wondering where we should go."

"Maybe we could just hang here for a while."

"Here? Are you serious? I thought you hated it here."

"It kinda grows on you. Besides, I love my job, and I hear that the dean of that new community college opening up in Taylorsville is just as queer as a football bat. Maybe you could get a gig there."

"Maybe." Being an openly gay English professor might not be so bad, Andie thought. But right now, as she pulled into the driveway, her career was the last thing on her mind. "Race you to the bedroom!"

Andie won the race only because Bev couldn't resist stopping for one split second to scratch kitty lang's furry head.

When Andie and Bev had made love previously,

they had taken turns pleasing each other, but now they were too ravenous, too passion-crazed to follow any set pattern. Frenzied, they tore at each other's clothes and fell upon each other, coming together in a blur of arms, thighs, fingers, breasts, tongues, lips, teeth, and sighs of 'I love you' and 'I missed you' and 'I missed this.' As they lay entwined in the big, soft bed, Andie couldn't help but think that the spirits of Eugenia Randall and Mildred Farmer were smiling down on them as the patron saints of women who choose to live together, work together, and love together.

The next morning, they were awakened by a knock on the door. Andie staggered out of bed and slipped into a robe. She opened the door to find Mamaw Needham, coatless in January, carrying a covered dish. "Why, Andie, honey, did I wake you up? Hit's awful late, ain't it?"

Andie cast a glance at the clock on the wall. It was 1:40 — not morning at all. Of course, they had been busy all night. "I guess it is."

"My daddy always said don't nobody need to get up no later than eight o'clock of a mornin' unless they've been up all night doin' somethin' they ain't s'posed to be doin'. Now, Andie, you ain't been doin' nothin' you ort not to, have you?"

Andie knew that Mamaw's joking was completely innocent, but she could still feel herself blushing. "Come on in, Mamaw."

"I finally brung you'uns that jam cake I told you'uns I'd make." Mamaw looked over Andie's shoulder, and Andie turned to see Bev standing in the doorway, wearing a T-shirt and boxer shorts, which was more than she had been wearing a few moments ago.

"Why, Beverly!" Mamaw Needham gushed. "Ain't you a sight for sore eyes."

"I guess I am," Bev laughed, running her fingers through her disheveled hair.

"Well, girls, I can't tell you how proud I am to see you'uns here together. You know, I never had no girls of my own, and since you'uns come here, I kinda took to thinkin' of you as my daughters. And I know it ain't none of my business about why you moved out or nothin', Beverly. But that night when you'uns come to supper, I could tell you'uns wasn't gettin' along."

"Well, I guess we were going through a rough patch," Andie said, taking Bev's hand. "But we're back together now."

"Well, I'm just real happy to hear that," Mamaw Needham said. "I always say that's how family ort to be — together. Now why don't I cut us all a piece of this jam cake?"

A few of the publications of
THE NAIAD PRESS, INC.
P.O. Box 10543 • Tallahassee, Florida 32302
Phone (904) 539-5965
Toll-Free Order Number: 1-800-533-1973
Mail orders welcome. Please include 15% postage.
Write or call for our free catalog which also features an incredible selection of lesbian videos.

HOODED MURDER by Annette Van Dyke. 176 pp. 1st Jessie Batelle Mystery. ISBN 1-56280-134-1 $10.95

WILDWOOD FLOWERS by Julia Watts. 208 pp. Hilarious and heart-warming tale of true love. ISBN 1-56280-127-9 10.95

NEVER SAY NEVER by Linda Hill. 224 pp. Rule #1: Never get involved with . . . ISBN 1-56280-126-0 10.95

THE SEARCH by Melanie McAllester. 240 pp. Exciting top cop Tenny Mendoza case. ISBN 1-56280-150-3 10.95

THE WISH LIST by Saxon Bennett. 192 pp. Romance through the years. ISBN 1-56280-125-2 10.95

FIRST IMPRESSIONS by Kate Calloway. 208 pp. P.I. Cassidy James' first case. ISBN 1-56280-133-3 10.95

OUT OF THE NIGHT by Kris Bruyer. 192 pp. Spine-tingling thriller. ISBN 1-56280-120-1 10.95

NORTHERN BLUE by Tracey Richardson. 224 pp. Police recruits Miki & Miranda — passion in the line of fire. ISBN 1-56280-118-X 10.95

LOVE'S HARVEST by Peggy Herring. 176 pp. by the author of *Once More With Feeling.* ISBN 1-56280-117-1 10.95

THE COLOR OF WINTER by Lisa Shapiro. 208 pp. Romantic love beyond your wildest dreams. ISBN 1-56280-116-3 10.95

FAMILY SECRETS by Laura DeHart Young. 208 pp. Enthralling romance and suspense. ISBN 1-56280-119-8 10.95

INLAND PASSAGE by Jane Rule. 288 pp. Tales exploring conventional & unconventional relationships. ISBN 0-930044-56-8 10.95

DOUBLE BLUFF by Claire McNab. 208 pp. 7th Detective Carol Ashton Mystery. ISBN 1-56280-096-5 10.95

BAR GIRLS by Lauran Hoffman. 176 pp. See the movie, read the book! ISBN 1-56280-115-5 10.95

THE FIRST TIME EVER edited by Barbara Grier & Christine Cassidy. 272 pp. Love stories by Naiad Press authors. ISBN 1-56280-086-8 14.95

MISS PETTIBONE AND MISS McGRAW by Brenda Weathers. 208 pp. A charming ghostly love story. ISBN 1-56280-151-1 10.95

CHANGES by Jackie Calhoun. 208 pp. Involved romance and relationships. ISBN 1-56280-083-3 10.95

FAIR PLAY by Rose Beecham. 256 pp. 3rd Amanda Valentine Mystery. ISBN 1-56280-081-7 10.95

PAXTON COURT by Diane Salvatore. 256 pp. Erotic and wickedly funny contemporary tale about the business of learning to live together. ISBN 1-56280-109-0 21.95

PAYBACK by Celia Cohen. 176 pp. A gripping thriller of romance, revenge and betrayal. ISBN 1-56280-084-1 10.95

THE BEACH AFFAIR by Barbara Johnson. 224 pp. Sizzling summer romance/mystery/intrigue. ISBN 1-56280-090-6 10.95

GETTING THERE by Robbi Sommers. 192 pp. Nobody does it like Robbi! ISBN 1-56280-099-X 10.95

FINAL CUT by Lisa Haddock. 208 pp. 2nd Carmen Ramirez Mystery. ISBN 1-56280-088-4 10.95

FLASHPOINT by Katherine V. Forrest. 256 pp. A Lesbian blockbuster! ISBN 1-56280-079-5 10.95

CLAIRE OF THE MOON by Nicole Conn. Audio Book —Read by Marianne Hyatt. ISBN 1-56280-113-9 16.95

FOR LOVE AND FOR LIFE: INTIMATE PORTRAITS OF LESBIAN COUPLES by Susan Johnson. 224 pp. ISBN 1-56280-091-4 14.95

DEVOTION by Mindy Kaplan. 192 pp. See the movie — read the book! ISBN 1-56280-093-0 10.95

SOMEONE TO WATCH by Jaye Maiman. 272 pp. 4th Robin Miller Mystery. ISBN 1-56280-095-7 10.95

GREENER THAN GRASS by Jennifer Fulton. 208 pp. A young woman — a stranger in her bed. ISBN 1-56280-092-2 10.95

TRAVELS WITH DIANA HUNTER by Regine Sands. Erotic lesbian romp. Audio Book (2 cassettes) ISBN 1-56280-107-4 16.95

CABIN FEVER by Carol Schmidt. 256 pp. Sizzling suspense and passion. ISBN 1-56280-089-1 10.95

THERE WILL BE NO GOODBYES by Laura DeHart Young. 192 pp. Romantic love, strength, and friendship. ISBN 1-56280-103-1 10.95

FAULTLINE by Sheila Ortiz Taylor. 144 pp. Joyous comic lesbian novel. ISBN 1-56280-108-2 9.95

OPEN HOUSE by Pat Welch. 176 pp. 4th Helen Black Mystery. ISBN 1-56280-102-3 10.95

ONCE MORE WITH FEELING by Peggy J. Herring. 240 pp. Lighthearted, loving romantic adventure. ISBN 1-56280-089-2 10.95

FOREVER by Evelyn Kennedy. 224 pp. Passionate romance — love overcoming all obstacles. ISBN 1-56280-094-9 10.95

WHISPERS by Kris Bruyer. 176 pp. Romantic ghost story ISBN 1-56280-082-5 10.95

NIGHT SONGS by Penny Mickelbury. 224 pp. 2nd Gianna Maglione Mystery. ISBN 1-56280-097-3 10.95

GETTING TO THE POINT by Teresa Stores. 256 pp. Classic southern Lesbian novel. ISBN 1-56280-100-7 10.95

PAINTED MOON by Karin Kallmaker. 224 pp. Delicious Kallmaker romance. ISBN 1-56280-075-2 10.95

THE MYSTERIOUS NAIAD edited by Katherine V. Forrest & Barbara Grier. 320 pp. Love stories by Naiad Press authors. ISBN 1-56280-074-4 14.95

DAUGHTERS OF A CORAL DAWN by Katherine V. Forrest. 240 pp. Tenth Anniversay Edition. ISBN 1-56280-104-X 10.95

BODY GUARD by Claire McNab. 208 pp. 6th Carol Ashton Mystery. ISBN 1-56280-073-6 10.95

CACTUS LOVE by Lee Lynch. 192 pp. Stories by the beloved storyteller. ISBN 1-56280-071-X 9.95

SECOND GUESS by Rose Beecham. 216 pp. 2nd Amanda Valentine Mystery. ISBN 1-56280-069-8 9.95

THE SURE THING by Melissa Hartman. 208 pp. L.A. earthquake romance. ISBN 1-56280-078-7 9.95

A RAGE OF MAIDENS by Lauren Wright Douglas. 240 pp. 6th Caitlin Reece Mystery. ISBN 1-56280-068-X 10.95

TRIPLE EXPOSURE by Jackie Calhoun. 224 pp. Romantic drama involving many characters. ISBN 1-56280-067-1 9.95

UP, UP AND AWAY by Catherine Ennis. 192 pp. Delightful romance. ISBN 1-56280-065-5 9.95

PERSONAL ADS by Robbi Sommers. 176 pp. Sizzling short stories. ISBN 1-56280-059-0 9.95

FLASHPOINT by Katherine V. Forrest. 256 pp. Lesbian blockbuster! ISBN 1-56280-043-4 22.95

CROSSWORDS by Penny Sumner. 256 pp. 2nd Victoria Cross Mystery. ISBN 1-56280-064-7 9.95

SWEET CHERRY WINE by Carol Schmidt. 224 pp. A novel of suspense. ISBN 1-56280-063-9 9.95

CERTAIN SMILES by Dorothy Tell. 160 pp. Erotic short stories. ISBN 1-56280-066-3 9.95

EDITED OUT by Lisa Haddock. 224 pp. 1st Carmen Ramirez Mystery. ISBN 1-56280-077-9 9.95

WEDNESDAY NIGHTS by Camarin Grae. 288 pp. Sexy adventure. ISBN 1-56280-060-4 10.95

SMOKEY O by Celia Cohen. 176 pp. Relationships on the playing field. ISBN 1-56280-057-4 9.95

KATHLEEN O'DONALD by Penny Hayes. 256 pp. Rose and Kathleen find each other and employment in 1909 NYC. ISBN 1-56280-070-1 9.95

STAYING HOME by Elisabeth Nonas. 256 pp. Molly and Alix want a baby . . . or do they? ISBN 1-56280-076-0 10.95

TRUE LOVE by Jennifer Fulton. 240 pp. Six lesbians searching for love in all the "right" places. ISBN 1-56280-035-3 10.95

GARDENIAS WHERE THERE ARE NONE by Molleen Zanger. 176 pp. Why is Melanie inextricably drawn to the old house? ISBN 1-56280-056-6 9.95

KEEPING SECRETS by Penny Mickelbury. 208 pp. 1st Gianna Maglione Mystery. ISBN 1-56280-052-3 9.95

THE ROMANTIC NAIAD edited by Katherine V. Forrest & Barbara Grier. 336 pp. Love stories by Naiad Press authors. ISBN 1-56280-054-X 14.95

UNDER MY SKIN by Jaye Maiman. 336 pp. 3rd Robin Miller Mystery. ISBN 1-56280-049-3. 10.95

STAY TOONED by Rhonda Dicksion. 144 pp. Cartoons — 1st collection since *Lesbian Survival Manual.* ISBN 1-56280-045-0 9.95

CAR POOL by Karin Kallmaker. 272pp. Lesbians on wheels and then some! ISBN 1-56280-048-5 10.95

NOT TELLING MOTHER: STORIES FROM A LIFE by Diane Salvatore. 176 pp. Her 3rd novel. ISBN 1-56280-044-2 9.95

GOBLIN MARKET by Lauren Wright Douglas. 240pp. 5th Caitlin Reece Mystery. ISBN 1-56280-047-7 10.95

LONG GOODBYES by Nikki Baker. 256 pp. 3rd Virginia Kelly Mystery. ISBN 1-56280-042-6 9.95

FRIENDS AND LOVERS by Jackie Calhoun. 224 pp. Midwestern Lesbian lives and loves. ISBN 1-56280-041-8 10.95

THE CAT CAME BACK by Hilary Mullins. 208 pp. Highly praised Lesbian novel. ISBN 1-56280-040-X 9.95

BEHIND CLOSED DOORS by Robbi Sommers. 192 pp. Hot, erotic short stories. ISBN 1-56280-039-6 9.95

CLAIRE OF THE MOON by Nicole Conn. 192 pp. See the movie — read the book! ISBN 1-56280-038-8 10.95

SILENT HEART by Claire McNab. 192 pp. Exotic Lesbian romance. ISBN 1-56280-036-1 10.95

HAPPY ENDINGS by Kate Brandt. 272 pp. Intimate conversations with Lesbian authors. ISBN 1-56280-050-7 10.95

THE SPY IN QUESTION by Amanda Kyle Williams. 256 pp. 4th Madison McGuire Mystery. ISBN 1-56280-037-X 9.95

SAVING GRACE by Jennifer Fulton. 240 pp. Adventure and romantic entanglement. ISBN 1-56280-051-5 9.95

THE YEAR SEVEN by Molleen Zanger. 208 pp. Women surviving in a new world. ISBN 1-56280-034-5 9.95

CURIOUS WINE by Katherine V. Forrest. 176 pp. Tenth Anniversary Edition. The most popular contemporary Lesbian love story. ISBN 1-56280-053-1 10.95

Audio Book (2 cassettes) ISBN 1-56280-105-8 16.95

CHAUTAUQUA by Catherine Ennis. 192 pp. Exciting, romantic adventure. ISBN 1-56280-032-9 9.95

A PROPER BURIAL by Pat Welch. 192 pp. 3rd Helen Black Mystery. ISBN 1-56280-033-7 9.95

SILVERLAKE HEAT: A Novel of Suspense by Carol Schmidt. 240 pp. Rhonda is as hot as Laney's dreams. ISBN 1-56280-031-0 9.95

LOVE, ZENA BETH by Diane Salvatore. 224 pp. The most talked about lesbian novel of the nineties! ISBN 1-56280-030-2 10.95

A DOORYARD FULL OF FLOWERS by Isabel Miller. 160 pp. Stories incl. 2 sequels to *Patience and Sarah.* ISBN 1-56280-029-9 9.95

MURDER BY TRADITION by Katherine V. Forrest. 288 pp. 4th Kate Delafield Mystery. ISBN 1-56280-002-7 10.95

THE EROTIC NAIAD edited by Katherine V. Forrest & Barbara Grier. 224 pp. Love stories by Naiad Press authors. ISBN 1-56280-026-4 14.95

DEAD CERTAIN by Claire McNab. 224 pp. 5th Carol Ashton Mystery. ISBN 1-56280-027-2 9.95

CRAZY FOR LOVING by Jaye Maiman. 320 pp. 2nd Robin Miller Mystery. ISBN 1-56280-025-6 9.95

STONEHURST by Barbara Johnson. 176 pp. Passionate regency romance. ISBN 1-56280-024-8 9.95

INTRODUCING AMANDA VALENTINE by Rose Beecham. 256 pp. 1st Amanda Valentine Mystery. ISBN 1-56280-021-3 9.95

UNCERTAIN COMPANIONS by Robbi Sommers. 204 pp. Steamy, erotic novel. ISBN 1-56280-017-5 9.95

A TIGER'S HEART by Lauren W. Douglas. 240 pp. 4th Caitlin Reece Mystery. ISBN 1-56280-018-3 9.95

PAPERBACK ROMANCE by Karin Kallmaker. 256 pp. A delicious romance. ISBN 1-56280-019-1 10.95

MORTON RIVER VALLEY by Lee Lynch. 304 pp. Lee Lynch at her best! ISBN 1-56280-016-7 9.95

THE LAVENDER HOUSE MURDER by Nikki Baker. 224 pp. 2nd Virginia Kelly Mystery. ISBN 1-56280-012-4 9.95

PASSION BAY by Jennifer Fulton. 224 pp. Passionate romance, virgin beaches, tropical skies. ISBN 1-56280-028-0 10.95

STICKS AND STONES by Jackie Calhoun. 208 pp. Contemporary lesbian lives and loves. ISBN 1-56280-020-5 9.95
Audio Book (2 cassettes) ISBN 1-56280-106-6 16.95

DELIA IRONFOOT by Jeane Harris. 192 pp. Adventure for Delia and Beth in the Utah mountains. ISBN 1-56280-014-0 9.95

UNDER THE SOUTHERN CROSS by Claire McNab. 192 pp. Romantic nights Down Under. ISBN 1-56280-011-6 9.95

GRASSY FLATS by Penny Hayes. 256 pp. Lesbian romance in the '30s. ISBN 1-56280-010-8 9.95

A SINGULAR SPY by Amanda K. Williams. 192 pp. 3rd Madison McGuire Mystery. ISBN 1-56280-008-6 8.95

THE END OF APRIL by Penny Sumner. 240 pp. 1st Victoria Cross Mystery. ISBN 1-56280-007-8 8.95

HOUSTON TOWN by Deborah Powell. 208 pp. A Hollis Carpenter Mystery. ISBN 1-56280-006-X 8.95

KISS AND TELL by Robbi Sommers. 192 pp. Scorching stories by the author of *Pleasures.* ISBN 1-56280-005-1 10.95

STILL WATERS by Pat Welch. 208 pp. 2nd Helen Black Mystery. ISBN 0-941483-97-5 9.95

TO LOVE AGAIN by Evelyn Kennedy. 208 pp. Wildly romantic love story. ISBN 0-941483-85-1 9.95

IN THE GAME by Nikki Baker. 192 pp. 1st Virginia Kelly Mystery. ISBN 1-56280-004-3 9.95

AVALON by Mary Jane Jones. 256 pp. A Lesbian Arthurian romance. ISBN 0-941483-96-7 9.95

STRANDED by Camarin Grae. 320 pp. Entertaining, riveting adventure. ISBN 0-941483-99-1 9.95

THE DAUGHTERS OF ARTEMIS by Lauren Wright Douglas. 240 pp. 3rd Caitlin Reece Mystery. ISBN 0-941483-95-9 9.95

CLEARWATER by Catherine Ennis. 176 pp. Romantic secrets of a small Louisiana town. ISBN 0-941483-65-7 8.95

THE HALLELUJAH MURDERS by Dorothy Tell. 176 pp. 2nd Poppy Dillworth Mystery. ISBN 0-941483-88-6 8.95

SECOND CHANCE by Jackie Calhoun. 256 pp. Contemporary Lesbian lives and loves. ISBN 0-941483-93-2 9.95

BENEDICTION by Diane Salvatore. 272 pp. Striking, contemporary romantic novel. ISBN 0-941483-90-8 9.95

BLACK IRIS by Jeane Harris. 192 pp. Caroline's hidden past . . . ISBN 0-941483-68-1 8.95

TOUCHWOOD by Karin Kallmaker. 240 pp. Loving, May/December romance. ISBN 0-941483-76-2 9.95

COP OUT by Claire McNab. 208 pp. 4th Carol Ashton Mystery. ISBN 0-941483-84-3 9.95

THE BEVERLY MALIBU by Katherine V. Forrest. 288 pp. 3rd Kate Delafield Mystery. ISBN 0-941483-48-7 10.95

THAT OLD STUDEBAKER by Lee Lynch. 272 pp. Andy's affair with Regina and her attachment to her beloved car. ISBN 0-941483-82-7 9.95

PASSION'S LEGACY by Lori Paige. 224 pp. Sarah is swept into the arms of Augusta Pym in this delightful historical romance. ISBN 0-941483-81-9 8.95

THE PROVIDENCE FILE by Amanda Kyle Williams. 256 pp. 2nd Madison McGuire Mystery. ISBN 0-941483-92-4 8.95

I LEFT MY HEART by Jaye Maiman. 320 pp. 1st Robin Miller Mystery. ISBN 0-941483-72-X 10.95

THE PRICE OF SALT by Patricia Highsmith (writing as Claire Morgan). 288 pp. Classic lesbian novel, first issued in 1952 . . . acknowledged by its author under her own, very famous, name. ISBN 1-56280-003-5 9.95

SIDE BY SIDE by Isabel Miller. 256 pp. From beloved author of *Patience and Sarah.* ISBN 0-941483-77-0 9.95

STAYING POWER: LONG TERM LESBIAN COUPLES by Susan E. Johnson. 352 pp. Joys of coupledom. ISBN 0-941-483-75-4 14.95

SLICK by Camarin Grae. 304 pp. Exotic, erotic adventure. ISBN 0-941483-74-6 9.95

NINTH LIFE by Lauren Wright Douglas. 256 pp. 2nd Caitlin Reece Mystery. ISBN 0-941483-50-9 8.95

PLAYERS by Robbi Sommers. 192 pp. Sizzling, erotic novel. ISBN 0-941483-73-8 9.95

MURDER AT RED ROOK RANCH by Dorothy Tell. 224 pp. 1st Poppy Dillworth Mystery. ISBN 0-941483-80-0 8.95

LESBIAN SURVIVAL MANUAL by Rhonda Dicksion. 112 pp. Cartoons! ISBN 0-941483-71-1 8.95

A ROOM FULL OF WOMEN by Elisabeth Nonas. 256 pp. Contemporary Lesbian lives. ISBN 0-941483-69-X 9.95

THEME FOR DIVERSE INSTRUMENTS by Jane Rule. 208 pp. Powerful romantic lesbian stories. ISBN 0-941483-63-0 8.95

CLUB 12 by Amanda Kyle Williams. 288 pp. Espionage thriller featuring a lesbian agent! ISBN 0-941483-64-9 8.95

DEATH DOWN UNDER by Claire McNab. 240 pp. 3rd Carol Ashton Mystery. ISBN 0-941483-39-8 9.95

MONTANA FEATHERS by Penny Hayes. 256 pp. Vivian and Elizabeth find love in frontier Montana. ISBN 0-941483-61-4 8.95

LIFESTYLES by Jackie Calhoun. 224 pp. Contemporary Lesbian lives and loves. ISBN 0-941483-57-6 10.95

WILDERNESS TREK by Dorothy Tell. 192 pp. Six women on vacation learning "new" skills. ISBN 0-941483-60-6 8.95

MURDER BY THE BOOK by Pat Welch. 256 pp. 1st Helen Black Mystery. ISBN 0-941483-59-2 9.95

THERE'S SOMETHING I'VE BEEN MEANING TO TELL YOU Ed. by Loralee MacPike. 288 pp. Gay men and lesbians coming out to their children. ISBN 0-941483-44-4 9.95

LIFTING BELLY by Gertrude Stein. Ed. by Rebecca Mark. 104 pp. Erotic poetry. ISBN 0-941483-51-7 10.95

AFTER THE FIRE by Jane Rule. 256 pp. Warm, human novel by this incomparable author. ISBN 0-941483-45-2 8.95

THREE WOMEN by March Hastings. 232 pp. Golden oldie. A triangle among wealthy sophisticates. ISBN 0-941483-43-6 8.95

PLEASURES by Robbi Sommers. 204 pp. Unprecedented eroticism. ISBN 0-941483-49-5 8.95

EDGEWISE by Camarin Grae. 372 pp. Spellbinding adventure. ISBN 0-941483-19-3 9.95

FATAL REUNION by Claire McNab. 224 pp. 2nd Carol Ashton Mystery. ISBN 0-941483-40-1 10.95

IN EVERY PORT by Karin Kallmaker. 228 pp. Jessica's sexy, adventuresome travels. ISBN 0-941483-37-7 10.95

OF LOVE AND GLORY by Evelyn Kennedy. 192 pp. Exciting WWII romance. ISBN 0-941483-32-0 10.95

CLICKING STONES by Nancy Tyler Glenn. 288 pp. Love transcending time. ISBN 0-941483-31-2 9.95

SOUTH OF THE LINE by Catherine Ennis. 216 pp. Civil War adventure. ISBN 0-941483-29-0 8.95

WOMAN PLUS WOMAN by Dolores Klaich. 300 pp. Supurb Lesbian overview. ISBN 0-941483-28-2 9.95

THE FINER GRAIN by Denise Ohio. 216 pp. Brilliant young college lesbian novel. ISBN 0-941483-11-8 8.95

OCTOBER OBSESSION by Meredith More. Josie's rich, secret Lesbian life. ISBN 0-941483-18-5 8.95

BEFORE STONEWALL: THE MAKING OF A GAY AND LESBIAN COMMUNITY by Andrea Weiss & Greta Schiller. 96 pp., 25 illus. ISBN 0-941483-20-7 7.95

OSTEN'S BAY by Zenobia N. Vole. 204 pp. Sizzling adventure romance set on Bonaire. ISBN 0-941483-15-0 8.95

LESSONS IN MURDER by Claire McNab. 216 pp. 1st Carol Ashton Mystery. ISBN 0-941483-14-2 9.95

YELLOWTHROAT by Penny Hayes. 240 pp. Margarita, bandit, kidnaps Julia. ISBN 0-941483-10-X 8.95

SAPPHISTRY: THE BOOK OF LESBIAN SEXUALITY by Pat Califia. 3d edition, revised. 208 pp. ISBN 0-941483-24-X 10.95

CHERISHED LOVE by Evelyn Kennedy. 192 pp. Erotic Lesbian love story. ISBN 0-941483-08-8 10.95

THE SECRET IN THE BIRD by Camarin Grae. 312 pp. Striking, psychological suspense novel. ISBN 0-941483-05-3 8.95

TO THE LIGHTNING by Catherine Ennis. 208 pp. Romantic Lesbian 'Robinson Crusoe' adventure. ISBN 0-941483-06-1 8.95

DREAMS AND SWORDS by Katherine V. Forrest. 192 pp. Romantic, erotic, imaginative stories. ISBN 0-941483-03-7 10.95

MEMORY BOARD by Jane Rule. 336 pp. Memorable novel about an aging Lesbian couple. ISBN 0-941483-02-9 10.95

THE ALWAYS ANONYMOUS BEAST by Lauren Wright Douglas. 224 pp. 1st Caitlin Reece Mystery. ISBN 0-941483-04-5 8.95

THE BLACK AND WHITE OF IT by Ann Allen Shockley. 144 pp. Short stories. ISBN 0-930044-96-7 7.95

SAY JESUS AND COME TO ME by Ann Allen Shockley. 288 pp. Contemporary romance. ISBN 0-930044-98-3 8.95

MURDER AT THE NIGHTWOOD BAR by Katherine V. Forrest. 240 pp. 2nd Kate Delafield Mystery. ISBN 0-930044-92-4 10.95

WINGED DANCER by Camarin Grae. 228 pp. Erotic Lesbian adventure story. ISBN 0-930044-88-6 8.95

PAZ by Camarin Grae. 336 pp. Romantic Lesbian adventurer with the power to change the world. ISBN 0-930044-89-4 8.95

SOUL SNATCHER by Camarin Grae. 224 pp. A puzzle, an adventure, a mystery — Lesbian romance. ISBN 0-930044-90-8 8.95

THE LOVE OF GOOD WOMEN by Isabel Miller. 224 pp. Long-awaited new novel by the author of the beloved *Patience and Sarah.* ISBN 0-930044-81-9 8.95

THE HOUSE AT PELHAM FALLS by Brenda Weathers. 240 pp. Suspenseful Lesbian ghost story. ISBN 0-930044-79-7 7.95

HOME IN YOUR HANDS by Lee Lynch. 240 pp. More stories from the author of *Old Dyke Tales.* ISBN 0-930044-80-0 7.95

PEMBROKE PARK by Michelle Martin. 256 pp. Derring-do and daring romance in Regency England. ISBN 0-930044-77-0 7.95

THE LONG TRAIL by Penny Hayes. 248 pp. Vivid adventures of two women in love in the old west. ISBN 0-930044-76-2 8.95

AN EMERGENCE OF GREEN by Katherine V. Forrest. 288 pp. Powerful novel of sexual discovery. ISBN 0-930044-69-X 10.95

THE LESBIAN PERIODICALS INDEX edited by Claire Potter. 432 pp. Author & subject index. ISBN 0-930044-74-6 12.95

DESERT OF THE HEART by Jane Rule. 224 pp. A classic; basis for the movie *Desert Hearts.* ISBN 0-930044-73-8 10.95

TORCHLIGHT TO VALHALLA by Gale Wilhelm. 128 pp. Classic novel by a great Lesbian writer. ISBN 0-930044-68-1 7.95

LESBIAN NUNS: BREAKING SILENCE edited by Rosemary Curb and Nancy Manahan. 432 pp. Unprecedented autobiographies of religious life. ISBN 0-930044-62-2 9.95

THE SWASHBUCKLER by Lee Lynch. 288 pp. Colorful novel set in Greenwich Village in the sixties. ISBN 0-930044-66-5 8.95

SEX VARIANT WOMEN IN LITERATURE by Jeannette Howard Foster. 448 pp. Literary history. ISBN 0-930044-65-7 8.95

A HOT-EYED MODERATE by Jane Rule. 252 pp. Hard-hitting essays on gay life; writing; art. ISBN 0-930044-57-6 7.95

AMATEUR CITY by Katherine V. Forrest. 224 pp. 1st Kate Delafield Mystery. ISBN 0-930044-55-X 10.95

THE SOPHIE HOROWITZ STORY by Sarah Schulman. 176 pp. Engaging novel of madcap intrigue. ISBN 0-930044-54-1 7.95

THE YOUNG IN ONE ANOTHER'S ARMS by Jane Rule. 224 pp. Classic Jane Rule. ISBN 0-930044-53-3 9.95

OLD DYKE TALES by Lee Lynch. 224 pp. Extraordinary stories of our diverse Lesbian lives. ISBN 0-930044-51-7 8.95

These are just a few of the many Naiad Press titles — we are the oldest and largest lesbian/feminist publishing company in the world. Please request a complete catalog. We offer personal service; we encourage and welcome direct mail orders from individuals who have limited access to bookstores carrying our publications.